Dedication

This book is dedicated to Robert Young, my father figure who is a consistent positive presence in my life

Acknowledgements

I would like to extend my sincere gratitude to the following Comox Valley businesses and organizations for their generous participation in this book:

•The K'ómoks First Nation branch, for their openness and invaluable insights

•Artful: The Gallery

•Midland Tools

•The Curry Cottage

•Tidal Café

•Island Affair Giftware

•Good's Groceries

•West Coast Karma

•Comox Library (with special thanks to Natalie)

•Courtenay Library

Finally, a heartfelt thank you to Mary, the remarkable K'ómoks woman whose story lies at the heart of this book. May your memory continue to illuminate truth and inspire learning for generations to come.

Dancing Mary

The Paranormal Canadiana Collection

Jay Lang-Young

Print ISBNs
Amazon print 9780228635277
Ingram Spark 9780228635284
Barnes & Noble 9780228635291
BWL Print 9780228635222

Copyright 2025 by Jay Lang
Editor JL Cartwright and JD Shipton
Cover artist Michelle Lee

The Paranormal Canadiana Collection

Night at the Legislature – Manitoba – Author Nancy M. Bell

Shúhta Dene – Northwest Territories – author Maureen Gresl

Astrophobia – Saskatchewan – author Paul Grant

Dancing Mary – British Columbia – author Jay Lang Young

Twice born – New Brunswick – author Graeme Smith

Playtime – Prince Edward Island – author Eden Monroe

2026 Releases

Ghosts of Bell Island - Newfoundland - Eileen Charbonneau and Jude Pittman

Black Gold Eye - Alberta – author JD Shipton

Haunting the Klondike - Yukon – author Joan Donaldson-Yarmey

Cardinal - Nova Scotia – author donalee Moulton

The Deepest Divide - Ontario – JC Kavanagh

Metamorphe - Quebec – author Juliet Waldron with John Wisdomkeeper (posthumously)

Table of Contents

Chapter One

The image of Laura's twisted body lying in a pool of blood flashes through my mind, too vivid, too raw, and I slam on the brakes. My heart races as I look up to see the ferryman in his yellow raincoat, holding an orange baton motioning me to resume driving up the creaking metal planks onto the first deck. Sweat beads across my forehead as I pull behind the parked vehicle in front of me and turn off the engine.

"Thank God! You were driving like a weirdo," scoffs Olivia, my fifteen-year-old daughter sitting in the passenger seat next to me. I sigh audibly and release my unintentional tight grasp on the wheel.

"Are you freaking out or something?" she says, shaking her head with disgust.

I feign a smile. "Of course not. What makes you say that?"

"Gee, I don't know. Maybe because you suddenly stopped the car half way onto the ferry and your face is frozen and sweating like a zombie."

"I think you're being a little dramatic, Olivia. And do zombies sweat?" I say, hoping to interject some levity into the moment.

"Forget it." She retorts, "I'm going upstairs." With one motion, she grabs the door handle and quickly jumps out.

"Be careful. Vehicles are still loading onto the..." My words are cut short by the slamming of the door.

Knowing she's safe within the confines of the ferry, I'm not so much worried about her finding trouble—something that's been a constant fear ever since her mother died two months ago. But as much as she's been a source of anxiety, she's also been a lifeline. While I've stressed over her making reckless choices out of grief, it's kept my mind occupied, pulling me away from the ever-present weight of my own struggle. In worrying about her, I've found something to cling to, instead of falling deeper into the darkness of my own depression.

The loud welcome aboard announcement blasts through the speakers throughout the ferry, reminding all vehicle passengers to exit their vehicles and make their way to the upper decks. I draw a deep breath into my lungs and twist the rear-view mirror to see my tired, drawn-out face and disheveled hair. If Laura were here, she'd be reaching her hand into her bag and pulling out a comb.

A portly trucker wearing a plaid work jacket walks past my window and nods. I have no choice, as much as I'd rather remain in the car for the duration of the sailing, it's not permitted and the last thing I want is to have one of the ship's workers come up and give me stress for not following the rules.

As I ascend the long metal stairwell, the ferry horn blasts, and I feel the boat shift as it pulls away from the Horseshoe Bay wharf. My hand instinctively grips the railing, steadying myself as I push forward. A knot tightens in my stomach at the thought of the trip ahead crossing the Georgia Strait, notorious for its turbulence, especially in Fall. I've never been a strong sailor. Since childhood, motion sickness has plagued me, and to my father's frustration, countless sea trips were canceled because of my weakness on the water.

As I step through the open door onto the upper bridge, the scent of freshly brewed coffee mixes with the makeshift cafeteria food being served nearby. I walk down the aisle, past passengers seated by large plexiglass windows, their eyes fixed on the turbulent grey sea. My gaze sweeps over each face, searching for the gothic figure Olivia has become. I can't help but feel a pang of guilt, embarrassed at times by how she makes me feel when we're in public. She resembles one of the characters from The Addams Family, a stark contrast to the bubbly child I once knew. Sometimes, I catch myself staring at her, desperately trying to find any trace of that carefree little girl who used to be my daughter. Still, I hold onto the hope that this trip will be more than just an obligation—it will be a connection back to each other. I believe that once Olivia releases Laura's ashes into the ocean, something inside her will shift. The anger that has consumed her for two long months will give way to acceptance, to peace with what happened. Maybe then, the distance between us will close, and we can begin to heal, both of us.

The movement of jet-black hair catches my eye in the cafeteria seating area. Olivia sits with her head buried deep inside a magazine at a lone table at the back of the open room. Maneuvering around the other passengers, I make my way to her table.

"Not eating, hunny?"

She doesn't look up. "If I wanted food, I would have gotten something," she answers, her voice muffled by the pages of the book.

"Well, I think I'm going to get myself a coffee," I say in an upbeat tone. "Are you sure I can't get you anything?"

Her severely lined eyes peer over the pages, shooting bullets into me. "It's like you don't hear a word I say," she snaps.

I momentarily close my eyes and gather my strength before leaning in closer to her. "Olivia, there's no need to escalate things all the time. It would be nice if you put some effort into getting along."

She stares at me with a venomous glare. "If you insist on sitting with me, just make sure you don't embarrass me!"

My eyes widen in disbelief. Embarrass her? Is she serious? I look like a cross between a stuffy lawyer and an accountant. Her, on the other hand, looks like she's just won the trophy at a Halloween costume party.

After getting myself a cup of what I would imagine is served in major institutions like prisons and hospitals, I make my way back to the table, dreading the next hour and a half with little miss sunshine. The ferry begins to sway as we enter the open water of Georgia Strait, and almost immediately, my stomach follows the motion with an uncomfortable lurch. I try to distract myself by focusing on the other passengers, keeping my gaze away from the choppy sea outside. A family of four catches my eye as they carefully navigate the aisles with their food trays, heading toward a nearby table. The father, about my age, looks clean-cut and conservative—not the usual laid-back Island type. His wife, also around the same age, is barking orders at their children—a twelve-year-old boy and a girl about Olivia's age.

They sit down, and without a word to each other, they begin eating, their attention fixed entirely on their phones—completely detached from one another and their surroundings. A sign of the times. I glance over at Olivia, who is either lost in whatever she's reading or deliberately avoiding me.

I'm not sure what's worse, being ignored by her or being the target of her venom when she does decide to speak to me.

* * *

We are one of the last vehicles off of the ferry after a long and nauseating sailing. Thankfully, I didn't throw up as the boat heaved from side to side. On a rough trip to Victoria a few years back, Laura had shown me a useful tip to help with my queasy stomach, "Focus on the horizon," she said. On that trip, it worked wonders, on this one, not so much.

"How long is the drive to Comox? I hate being stuck in this stupid car," Olivia snaps.

I tell her it's about an hour and fifteen minutes, hoping, if I'm lucky, she'll fall asleep and spare me her grim attitude. As we turn north onto the Island Highway, my thoughts drift to Laura's mother and the few relatives she had on the Island. I wonder about Greta—Laura's mom, a cold Dutch woman I met only once, at our wedding in Kitsilano. From what Laura told me, they were never close, mostly because Laura refused to conform to her mother's rigid religious beliefs. Apparently, Laura's dad had the same cold nature as his wife, which pushed Laura to make the choice to leave home when she was still a teenager. She worked three jobs while attending UBC, paying her own rent and tuition without any help from her parents. An English Major in the Honors Program, Laura had intended to become a teacher—but that never happened. We met through mutual friends before she graduated, and before we knew it, she was pregnant with Olivia. I was a junior lawyer at the time and although I wasn't making great money, I did have a healthy nest egg thanks to an inheritance from my grandfather and money I had saved from working at my fathers accounting office. Laura didn't need to work if she didn't want to, which she didn't. Her whole focus was our unborn child and how she wanted to dedicate all of her time to becoming the parent she never had. Not long after Olivia was born, I hit what would be considered the jackpot of jobs, landing a position at a prestigious law firm in downtown Vancouver—it was the break I needed that set me up to be part of a winning team and build my credentials as a worthy securities lawyer.

Soon, we moved out of our small two-bedroom apartment on Cardero Street and bought a wonderful heritage home in the upscale Shaunessy neighborhood. If only we would've stayed in that house, that area, where Olivia attended private school and had good friends, where life was more manageable, maybe Laura would still be alive and Olivia wouldn't have gone down the dark path she is on.

A loud blast from a horn shocks me away from my thoughts and causes me to jump.

"Dad. Are you serious right now?"

I look over at my daughter who is staring at me disapprovingly.

"What's the problem?" I say, noticing a white truck in the rear-view mirror.

"Don't you think you should speed up? You're not even going the speed limit." She says, leaning over to look at the speedometer. "The speed limit is 100 and you're only going 90.

I tell Olivia the truck can pass me if he doesn't like the speed I'm driving, since there are two other lanes. Sure enough, the guy eventually speeds up and flips me the bird as he whizzes by—early 20s, wearing a backward baseball cap.

Olivia sinks lower in her seat, making it clear how embarrassed she is by the whole situation. There are times, moments like these, when I want to yell at her, snap her out of her dramatics and rudeness. But since her mother died, Olivia's been on this strange, self-destructive path, and the last thing I want is to be the one who pushes her over the edge. I'm still holding on to the hope that she'll find a way out of the dark place she's stuck in.

Chapter Two

Comox is a charming little town, where the retirement age seems to outnumber the rest of the population. The main road, Comox Ave, runs parallel to the sea and is lined with small, quaint shops and restaurants that stretch along both sides of the narrow two-lane road. Using the nav-tech to find the address of the rental home I booked; we drive up a winding lane flanked by towering Douglas Fir and Spruce trees.

Olivia cracks her window, and a mix of fresh sea air and the raw scent of nature flows into the car. We turn down a gravel side driveway, and after a few moments, the house comes into view—a three-story A-frame nestled in a blanket of trees, perched high on a bluff.

I pop the trunk and we get out of the car. "What do you think? It's pretty nice, huh?" I ask, pulling our bags from the back.

Olivia shrugs. "It looks like a doghouse on steroids."

I shake my head and continue unloading the car.

After toting our bags to the front step and retrieving the key under the matt, we walk inside. The house is stunning, with an open concept layout, beautiful wood floors, and windows that stretch from floor to ceiling. Modern appliances and stylish accents make it a perfect blend of contemporary comfort and rustic charm—just as the online ad promised.

"Where is my room?" Olvia stands in the middle of the floor with her shoulders slumped, grasping onto the handle of her suitcase.

"Pick whichever room you like. There's a great loft that is supposed to get a lot of sunlight."

"Isn't there a basement?"

"Nope. This is an A-Frame house, no dark basement, I'm afraid. I guess you'll have to exist in the light with the rest of human beings." I snicker.

"You're a riot, Dad." She says, turning her back to me and walking up the spiral wooden staircase.

I make a few more trips to the car for bags and my briefcase, even though I've already told my office I'm not planning on doing much work while I'm here. Still, I'll need to check in with my associates online now and then. I'm a little apprehensive about not working. Without the distraction of being buried in a case, who knows what my mind will do. I've struggled to process everything that happened. Instead of finding answers, I've only accumulated more questions: Why did she jump? Was her life really that bad? Why didn't she come to me first?

"Dad, I hope you know that there's only one bathroom up here!"

I glance up to the floor above where Olivia is leaning on the railing, looking down at me with complete horror.

"You do understand that I need my own bathroom, right?"

"There's supposed to be another one down here somewhere, so don't worry."

"Fine!" she says, disappearing into a doorway.

A part of me feels resentful toward Laura for leaving me with the aftermath of what she did. Olivia was always polite and loving before her mother's death. Now, she's as dark inside as the black clothing she wears. And I have no idea how to help her. And something tells me that Laura's family isn't going to be much benefit emotionally to me or my daughter.

* * *

It's 7 a.m. when I'm jolted awake by hard rapping on the door. Grabbing my housecoat, I slip it on and shuffle down the narrow spiral stairs. I make my way through the foyer and head to the door and look out of the glass.

A slender man, dressed in casual clothes and a baseball cap, stands on the first step. I cover a yawn with the back of my hand, make sure my robe is covering me properly, and open the door.

"Can I help you?"

He introduces himself as the owner and mentions there's been a terrible mistake. Apparently, the house was accidentally overbooked—a huge oversight by his wife.

"The other party is flying in from the U.K. and landing at Comox airport in about three hours," he says, glancing at his watch. "They booked the house months ago." He looks apologetic and embarrassed.

I sigh. "This kind of puts me in a jam. I'm not sure what to do now. And my daughter is sleeping upstairs."

"I'm so sorry. However, I may have a solution. We own another rental property right at the top of Dyke Road, just as you come into Comox. It's a two-bedroom log cabin with a fireplace and a big patio overlooking the water. It's really nice. And because of the mix-up, the first week's rent is on us." He looks at me, hopeful.

Seeing no way out of the predicament, I agree to his offer and tell him we'll be out of the house in an hour. The landlord hands me a set of keys along with the address to the new place, and I close the door, dreading the task of waking up the dark force who's sleeping upstairs. Regardless of the fact that I have no control over the situation, I'll be blamed and this will be just one more awful thing I've done or let happen to her. Great, just great!

* * *

As predicted, Olivia spazzed out at the news of our impromptu change of plans and practically threw her suitcase down the stairs. The last words she spoke before committing to not speaking to me were, "I can't even stand riding in this car right now." I wanted to suggest that she fly her broom instead and I would meet her at the new place, but I knew the joke would be lost on her and inevitably would only cause more tension.

During the silent ride down Comox Ave, I turn onto Beach Drive until we come to a narrow driveway with the address on the side of a mailbox. The road is bumpy and overgrown with rogue branches that scrape along the side of my car. Finally, we pull up to a one-level cabin with a large painted sign over a white, paint-chipped door. "Seabreeze Cabin."

"Ha! Are you serious? This is the place? I hope they're not charging us!" Olivia finally speaks.

"Have a positive attitude. I'm sure it will be fine."

She scoffs as I turn off the engine, then gets out of the car and slams the door. I'm not sure how much more of her behavior I can take. I've done everything I can to accommodate her mood swings, but like a pressure cooker, I can feel the tension building in me.

Before removing our luggage from the trunk, I open the door, and we step inside. Thankfully, it's nice—quite deceiving compared to the aged exterior of the building. Olivia immediately walks through the place, opening every door down the only hallway off the living room, surveying or mentally critiquing every flaw, I'm sure. I peruse the main area of the house and am relieved to see the new appliances, a spacious living room, and a view that far surpasses the one at the A-frame house we just left.

Olivia hollers from down the hall, "Well, at least there are two bedrooms, though with all the wood in this place, I'm sure there are going to be tons of spiders."

I smile and shake my head, then tell her to come and get her bags from the car.

* * *

After setting up our rooms, we head to Courtenay to pick up groceries for the day. While flipping through The Comox Free Press on the ferry, I stumble upon an article about an Asian/Mexican store called Goods Grocery in the Valley.

When we step into Goods Grocery, we're immediately greeted by Mark and Glenda Turner, the owners. Both are warm and welcoming, with a wealth of knowledge about the eclectic range of products they carry—everything from snacks and sweets to an impressive variety of ingredients for any culinary need. An elderly customer walks in and strikes up a conversation with Olivia, asking where we're from and how long we'll be visiting the area. Thankfully, my daughter reserves her verbal jabs for me and keeps things polite with the woman.

"You should meet up with some of the local teens at the Youth Center in town while you're visiting. I'm sure you'll find kids your age there, "the woman says.

I can tell by the dismissive look in Olivia's eyes that a youth center is the last place she'd consider visiting. I can't say I blame her, we're not tourists looking to see the sights. Our reason for coming to the valley is far more depressing and personal. After we gather our groceries, we're just heading out of the store when I notice Olivia's attention shift to a group of goth looking teens leaning against the outside of the building. Dressed in either dark or muted straggly clothes, from what I can see, they all have face piercings and black hair. They stand out like a sore thumb against the aesthetics of the area, but then again, so does Olivia.

Chapter Three

The northern wind pushes hard against the old windows, causing the glass to shutter noisily in the frames. I walk over and look out into the dark night. White caps crest over the churning sea, glowing on top of the rising waves. In the safety of the house, I appreciate the beauty of the scene. If I were on the ferry, I'd be ill with seasickness and unable to appreciate how magnificent the ocean looks—a moving painting before me. For a brief moment, I think about calling Olivia, who's been holed up in her room, so she can see how amazing the water looks, but I'm not sure if she'd appreciate it the same way.

That being said, it is a dark and somewhat macabre scene I'm looking at, so you'd think Olivia could relate. Still, I opt to leave her alone. I'm just about to turn away from the window when I think I see a light briefly flicker from the shore. Stepping closer to the glass, I focus intently on the water's edge—nothing. I guess my eyes are playing tricks on me. After all, I've had a few more glasses of wine than I intended, and to top it off, I'm emotionally drained.

I shut off the lights, check the door lock, and head to bed. Once my head hits the pillow, I make a mental note to make the call I've been dreading since we arrived in the Comox Valley—to Laura's mother.

* * *

The sound of screeching gulls fills the air above the cabin, their cries cutting through the silence and permeating the single-paned windows. I groan at the dull ache behind my eyes, a reminder to drink less wine before bed. By the time I've had a quick shower and gotten dressed, Olivia is already in the kitchen, slipping two pieces of bread into the toaster.

"Wow. I can't believe you're up before me," I say, still rubbing my eyes.

She shrugs, unfazed. "Yeah, well, I'm getting picked up in an hour, so I thought I'd eat something first."

I blink, confused, and stare at her. "Picked up?"

"Yep." She turns toward me with an almost smug look, her voice full of self-assurance. "My grandmother's coming to pick me up."

"What do you mean? How did you get in touch with her?" I ask, trying to process the information.

"I have her number, Dad. Mom gave it to me. Not that we talk much. Usually, only at Christmas or my birthday."

"Oh." I feel a lump form in my throat, a bit of anger creeping in. "Well, that's the first I'm hearing of this." I can't help but feel a little dejected, almost betrayed. It stings that neither Olivia nor her mother bothered to tell me about this sooner. "Just so you're aware, you are in fact a minor, and you need to ask me, your parent, for permission before you make plans to get picked up."

My words hang in the air, more of a sharp retort than a lesson.

Olivia plants her hands on her hips and tilts her head, her chin lifting in a defensive stance. "She's my family too. I don't see why I need to ask to go with family."

I take a deep breath, trying to steady myself. "You don't know her, Olivia. Maybe you've spoken to her on the phone a couple of times, but that's not the same thing. She's not someone you can just trust. You barely know this woman."

I want to warn Olivia about her so-called grandmother, about how she's the kind of person who's rigid in her beliefs, using them to manipulate and control, to try and convert people to her way of thinking. A mean-spirited woman who drove her own daughter out of the house. I can't shake the feeling that this could be a mistake. But instead, I swallow the words, knowing I need to tread carefully with Olivia.

"Where exactly are you going and when will you be back?"

She tells me that her grandmother is taking her to her house and she'll be back by dinner time. I reach for a cup in the cupboard as Olivia butters her toast. "Don't make plans again without speaking to me first."

"Whatever!" she snaps.

As I sit on the sofa and watch the calm sea, Olivia stomps around the cabin getting ready. In a way I'm worried for her, about what her grandmother may say. The woman was never a fan of mine. In her eyes, I was the reason her daughter never returned to the Valley, even though that couldn't be further from the truth. Gaslighting, I think it's called. When a guilty person blames someone else to take the focus off themselves.

* * *

I hear the honk of a car horn outside then the intentionally loud footsteps from Olivia as she makes her way to the front door.

"So, I guess I'll see you before dinner then?"

"Yep," she says, opening the door then shutting it hard behind her."

I hear the car leave then get up and walk to my room, noting the time on the living room clock and etching it in my mind. If my child is back here any later that 6 pm, I'm going to be pissed. Once in the bedroom, I see my cell on the edge of the dresser and decide to charge the battery, just in case Olivia decides she wants to come home sooner and needs to call me. I search for the charger in all of the usual places, my bag, the wall outlet and the kitchen counter but it's nowhere. Then, I remember that Olivia often swipes my charger and I have to go on a hunt to find it. I go to her room and slowly open the door; I don't want to disturb anything as it would be grounds for another argument between us. Spotting the charger on the side table nearest the window, I carefully avoid the mass of clothes and other obstacles strewn across the floor. Once I grab the charger, I turn to leave the room when I notice a strange gold symbol poking out from the inside of a hoodie on the bottom of the bed. I reach down and pull out a book with a shiny round design-gothic or pagan, I think but I'm not sure and the front cover has no text anywhere. I push over the hoodie and sit on the edge of the bed and open the book. It's a diary or a journal. Olivia's writing and drawings have covered most of the pages. I know I should put the book back and leave it where I found it but my desire to know what is in my kid's head exceeds any guilt I feel.

"These are my private thoughts and maybe by the end of this book, they will be the last ones I have."

My eyes widen in disbelief, is Olivia suicidal or are her words just an outburst from a hormonal teen? I read on. It doesn't take long for my question to be answered, Olivia is in trouble, real trouble. With every page I turn, words that echo the signs of a troubled mind jump off the page, witchcraft, dark spirits, spells and revenge are repeatedly mentioned. There are even strange recipes for concocting spells. It's all so unbelievable and strange. I take a deep breath and read on. From what I am learning, she is angry at her mother for leaving her, but she's furious with me. A poorly written poem talks about how I sealed her mother's fate by working too much and ignoring her. My heart grows heavy and a hard lump forms in my throat. Olivia's feelings echo my own. Laura was the love of my life, but I was never home to prove that to her. Instead, I showed my love for her by providing a beautiful home on some of the richest property in Vancouver. From expensive jewelry to fancy cars, I did everything to make sure that my wife never wanted for anything, only, she did. She wanted me but I was too busy working long hours at the firm. It was only after I found out that she had an affair, not out of love but out of sheer loneliness did I learn just how far apart Laura and I really were. The guilt is what killed my wife, long before she jumped from the penthouse balcony. She couldn't take the guilt over what she had done. Only, the guilt should never have been her burden, it was mine to carry. A tear rolls down my cheek and splashes on a page. I quickly wipe away the moisture and close the book, returning it exactly as I found it.

Chapter Four

Life throws us curve balls, it's just the way it is, everyone goes through tough times. But I bet there's not a lot of people going through the overwhelming amount of devastation and craziness that I've endured over just two short months. And to top it off, my once sweet child has turned into my biggest opponent. She's my judge and jury when it comes to what happened to her mother. And just to top it all off, she's now deep into witchcraft, something I've always believed fell in conjunction with the mentally disturbed. I'm not sure what to do to save her from the path she's walking down. Therapy won't do her much good, I learned that after her mother died, and I insisted on her getting some professional counselling. At $400 dollars an hour, it took three sessions for the therapist to tell me that Olivia was a closed book and wouldn't open up about her feelings at all.

Back in the living room, I sit motionless on the couch and stare out at the sea, depressed and defeated, I question our future.

A small flicker shines from the shore, like a mirror reflecting the sun. I slowly get up and walk over to the window. As soon as the flash disappears, I see the slender figure of a woman, her long dark hair blowing wildly in the ocean breeze. With her head down, she seems to be perusing the water line, walking along methodically staring at the ground. Curious. For some reason, I can't take my eyes off her as I watch her pace back and forth in one specific area. After about twenty minutes, I come to the conclusion that she's lost something and is intently searching for whatever it is. Not wanting to sit in the house with my racing thoughts, I decide to go for a walk on the shore. Maybe I can speak with the woman on the beach. Maybe she wants some help looking for what she lost. If not, at least I'll be out of the house and distracted from my heavy thoughts.

* * *

Walking along the narrow dirt path on the side of the house, I almost trip on a large root that's jetting out of the packed soil. Once I reach the sand, I look up to see if the woman is still by the waters edge—she is. As I make my way toward her, a thought enters my mind, what if I approach her and she thinks I'm a weirdo or a pervert? That couldn't be further from the truth but how will she know that? I should have thought this through better. I'm just about to turn around when the woman notices me and waves a friendly hello. At least I know she's not feeling creeped out by my presence. I continue to walk to the shore, only looking up a couple of times. But once I get close enough, I make eye contact. She's beautiful with her long chocolate hair and matching brown eyes. Her face is like a flawless sculpture with smooth, perfect skin and full pink lips. Now, I'm really nervous. I immediately feel self conscious and divert my attention to the water.

"Good morning." She says cheerfully .

"Hello." I respond, forcing myself to look at her.

She asks if I live around here, and I offer a response, "I'm staying at a cottage with my daughter, but I'm not sure how long we'll be in the Comox Valley." She tells me her name is Mary, and I introduce myself. When I return the question, asking if she lives here, she responds that she's lived in the area forever. I laugh and say she doesn't look old enough to have been here that long. She smiles and says it feels like she has.

From the few quick glances I steal when she's not looking, I place her in her early to mid-twenties—very young. But there's something older about her, though I can't quite put my finger on it. Maybe it's the way she carries herself, so confident and self-assured when she speaks. Then again, I suppose most beautiful women have that air about them, don't they? Eventually, her focus shifts from me back to the shoreline, her eyes scanning it with intense concentration, moving quickly from one spot to the next.

"Did you lose something?" I ask.

She frowns, "Yes. I lost something very precious to me, a necklace my mother gave to me."

"When did you lose it?"

Mary shrugs, "I can't be sure of the exact date, but it was a long time ago."

"I see. Well, two sets of eyes might double your chances, I'll help you search for it," I say, scanning the waters edge.

The wind picks up and causes a fine spray of sea water to hit us and makes our search harder. Not to mention, breakers are beginning to crash into shore and fill the waters edge with foam.

Mary smiles, "I guess mother nature has decided not to reveal my necklace to us today."

I laugh, "I'm sorry about that. I was really hoping we could find it."

"Don't worry, I'll find it one day. I come down here every day to search."

"Well, if I see you out here, I'll make sure to come and say hello and resume the search."

"That's very nice of you, Oliver. I appreciate the help." Mary shakes my hand; her skin is smooth and soft but as cold as ice.

"You'd better get home, you're freezing."

"It's a coastal thing. Cold hands, warm heart," she laughs.

And with that, we say our goodbyes and part ways.

As I enter the path at the side of the cabin, I turn back to look for my beautiful new friend but she has already vanished. I continue walking and smile, the whole time I was speaking with Mary, all of the intense stress I've been under seemed to disappear. Though, with each step closer to the cabin door, I can feel the tension growing again. By the time I'm back in the house, my mind is filled with worry and anxiety. Is Olivia alright? Has her crazy grand Greta been filling her head with negative lies about me, which would only add to the hostility my daughter feels toward me.

* * *

It's ten minutes after 5 when Olivia comes through the front door. I quickly put down my book and sprint to the door, hoping to catch Greta before she pulls out of the driveway. If she sees me wave, the gesture might redeem me somewhat for not calling her when we arrived in the Valley. But, just as I reach the door, the car headlights are obstructed by tree branches as the car backs up. Olivia kicks off her shoes as I fight the wind to close the door.

Without saying a word to me, Olivia starts walking toward her bedroom.

"How was your visit?"

She shrugs, "Fine."

I want to call her to come back and sit with me and then force her to open up to me about what happened while she was with her grandmother, what the old woman said, and more importantly, ask her why she wrote all of that strange sinister stuff in her journal, but I can't. I know that the more I push her, the more she'll push back. I guess I owe that character defect to myself, as I've always been the same way. Instead, I pour myself a glass of wine and stand at the window overlooking the sea, another stormy night with the whitecaps glowing as they dance on top of the rolling water.

Chapter Five

"Dad, is it okay if I meet up with some local kids after we have lunch? Olivia is looking out of the rain-soaked window in the passenger seat as I navigate our way to Tidal Café, a local eatery that came highly recommended on the Comox Facebook page.

I'm not sure what I'm more shocked about, Olivia speaking to me with out including an insult or the fact that she's being proactive and wants to get out and do things.

"What kids? You don't know anyone here."

In her usual 14 year old fashion, she slumps her shoulders and rolls her eyes, "Dad. I met some people on a local teen chat group. I even zoom called one of the girls and met her mother. It's totally safe, Dad."

I ask her what she plans on doing with her new friends and she huffs, "We were going to go and hang out at a coffee shop and talk and then maybe go to the library, that's it. They seem like good kids, so you wont have to worry about us planning any murders or anything."

I think about my next words as I want to keep the communication open while finding a way to maintain a responsible parent position.

"I'll tell you what, I'll let you go, but I want to drop you off so I can see who you're with."

I might as well have said that I was going to chain her up and tie her in her room forever based on how she responded. "You don't love me" and "All you want to do is treat me like a baby and embarrass me." Ending with her crossing her arms and shooting me an evil leer. , "Just forget I even asked."

Thankfully, the lady at Tidal Café was not only a great server but liked to converse so I had someone to talk to while Olivia receded into a combination of silence and resentment. I'm not sure if it's because I'm becoming desensitized to my daughters snarky disposition or what but regardless of her determination to be miserable, I was able to enjoy the scenery in the quaint café, along with the chats with the kindly waitress and the amazing food I ordered, A salmon benny on homemade biscuits. Olivia opted to have nothing in a feeble attempt to protest my request to meet her new friends. I wonder if other parents are enduring the teen angst stage with their kids. If so, I'm sure they would agree with me that having a teenager is a great form of birth control and makes you pretty much certain that you definitely don't want to jump into having another kid when they turn into evil little imps.

The ride home is much like the ride to the café, quiet and cold. The only difference is, the rain has stopped and the dark clouds have been replaced with one of the most vibrant and stunning rainbows I have ever seen.

* * *

The water lies unusually still, its surface mirroring the dark sky and it's millions of stars, blurring the line between the sea and heaven, where one seems to seamlessly merge into the other. It's incredible how quickly the weather can change here in the valley, from angry skies to complete calmness. With Olivia upstairs pouting in her room, I poured a scotch and was just taking my first sip when I saw a silhouette strolling slowly on the waters edge—Mary.

It's already 8:30 at night so I'm convinced I won't see Olivia until tomorrow morning when hopefully she will have shed some of her bad mood. With this is mind, I quickly walk to the front door, slide on my shoes, grab my coat and head out to talk with my pretty new friend.

This time, as my feet crunch softly over the small pebbles and sand, walking toward her—because we've already met—I don't worry about seeming like a creep in the night. A light from Courtenay spills across the water, and when Mary turns to face me, her silhouette shimmers with a soft, glowing blue, giving her an almost ethereal aura.

"You're out quite late." I smile.

She grins sweetly, "It's not so late, besides, I'm not much for sleeping."

I'm just about to ask her about her necklace and if she should try to broaden her search up the beach when she looks over my shoulder toward the woods, "You know, there used to be a small settlement there a long time ago."

I turn and look back the way I came. "Where?" I ask, looking at the lights coming from a group of apartment buildings.

"Never mind," she says. "Out with the old and in with the new, I guess." With that, she turns her attention to the waters edge as it ebbs and then slowly crawls back up the sand. As I help her search for her beloved jewelry, she asks me about Vancouver and what it's like there. I find it hard to believe that she's never been off of the Island but I leave it alone and don't ask too many personal questions, I don't know her well enough yet. We talk for what seems like minutes but ends up being a couple of hours when I look down at my watch. "It's getting late. You must be getting cold," I say. For a moment I consider inviting her back to the cabin for a drink or even just a warmer place to talk, but it doesn't feel right, it's too soon in our friendship. Besides, if Olivia did decide to leave the confines of her room and see me there with Mary, a younger beautiful woman, I'd never hear the end of it.

"I guess I should be going," she says softly.

I offer to walk her home and she giggles, "No thank you. I'm very capable of getting myself home. Besides, it's not far."

We walk together until the sand ends and the grass starts. After a quick goodbye, I tell her that I'll keep an eye out for her and if I see her on the beach, I'll come out again to help her search. She smiles then waves as she walks along a small path toward a wooded area.

Once back inside, I kick off my shoes and resume my seat on the couch where my drink still sits on the end table. I'm not sure if it's because of the sea air or the way Mary puts me at ease, but after my drink, I feel unusually tired and after shutting off the lights and checking the front door lock, I head to bed.

Nothing can prepare a parent for the moment their child goes missing. In an instant, everything within you unravels—rational thought, focus, and any semblance of calm vanish. What's left is a frantic panic, each breath consumed by a cascade of dreadful possibilities, spiraling from one nightmare to the next. This is exactly how I felt when I opened Olivia's door a few minutes ago and found only an unmade bed and the window ajar. My first thought is to call her grandmother, someone I probably should've called by now but I haven't got up the nerve, I've had my hands full trying to filter Olivia's negativity, let alone having to speak with a cold old bitter nag like Greta. I take a deep breath and scroll through my contacts list on my phone and then push send.

"Hello." Her voice has aged over the years and now sounds heavier and raspy.

"Greta," It's me, Oliver. I was just wondering if..."

"Oh, it's you!" she snaps. "not masking the fact she's unhappy to hear from me.

"Yes. It's me. Listen, Olivia is missing. I've just checked her room and…"

"Missing?" she interrupts again. "What do you mean?" she says, revealing hints of her European accent.

I quickly explain how Olivia isn't home and that I have no idea how long she has been gone. "I'm calling because I was hoping that maybe you've heard from her."

Greta tells me that she hasn't spoken to Olivia since she dropped her off at the cabin and then suggests that I go through my daughters room looking for anything like a diary or pieces of paper with someone's name on it. As much as I can't stand the old pat, she's got a great idea and immediately my head flashes back to Olivia's journal. From what I had read, she is big on writing things down, so maybe, just maybe she's left a clue to where she's gone. I tell Greta that I'll keep her posted and end the call.

I sprint down the hallway and burst into Olivia's room, my eyes immediately scanning for the strange-looking notebook. I rifle through the pile of clothes on the floor, then sift through her jackets and hoodies scattered across the bed—nothing. My anxiety spikes as I check the dresser drawers, but still, nothing. Disheartened and desperate, a rising panic fills me as the only thought that comes to mind is to call the police. I turn and rush back toward the front room, where I'd left my phone on the counter, but just as I reach it, I hear the knob on the front door rattle.

Praying it's my daughter, I sprint to the door and open it. There standing in front of me is my kid, disheveled and pale with exhaustion.

Olivia looks up at me sheepishly. "Sorry. I didn't want to wake you. I was hoping the door would be unlocked."

For a long moment, I'm speechless, staring at her in disbelief. Then, the parent in my kicks in. "Have you completely lost your mind?"

Olivia scoffs, "I'm not going to argue with you. I'm going to my room." She walks inside and attempts to veer around me. I catch a glimpse of her journal sticking out of her front hoodie pocket and quickly step in front of her, "Get your ass on the couch right now. We need to talk."

Her eyes widen in surprise, and I realize this might be the first time I've ever cursed at her. But it worked. She knows I'm serious, and without another word, she walks into the living room, slumps onto the sofa, and stares at the floor.

When I sit down beside her, I take a deep breath before launching into the dangers of running off in the middle of the night. I list every risk I can think of my voice sounding almost foreign to me, like the scolding I used to get from my parents when I was her age. And with that thought, I know that my words are falling on deafened ears. Just as the lectures from my mom and Dad had no real impact on me. After my futile speech, Olivia asks if she can go to her room and with no more for me to say, I tell her to call her grandmother to let her know she's safe.

I sit there, frustrated and alone, lost in thoughts of what the future holds—for me, a guilt-ridden widower, and for my child, a confused, grieving teenager. Without an open dialogue between us, I'm left scrambling for anything I can do to protect her. My mind quickly shifts to her journal. The moment she leaves it unattended, I'll sneak a glance at her recent entries, hoping to find some clue, some hint into what's swirling around in that troubled mind of hers.

Chapter Six

Spreading Laura's ashes was the whole reason we came to the island, to her hometown. But until this morning, I've done everything I can to avoid it. In some way, I guess I'm still holding on to her. After a long debate about where to set Laura free, Greta wanted her ashes scattered in the waters of Kye Bay, while I had my heart set on the inlet in front of our rental cabin—somewhere we could return to, where Laura's remains would always be close by. To my surprise, Olivia sided with me, and we won.

An old, withered woman, her exterior as bitter and unapproachable as her character—that's the first impression I have when I see Greta after all these years. Olivia, no doubt desperate to connect with her mother's bloodline, rushes to help Greta get out of the car.

"Hello," Greta. I say, putting on polite airs.

She grumbles without making eye contact then, with the help of my daughter, ambles around the cabin to the beach. With the bronze urn carrying my wife's ashes grasped firmly in my arms, we make our way around the cabin to the beach. The tide is high so thankfully with the sea closer, I don't have to worry about Greta navigating over slippery stones to the waters edge. Standing silent for a few minutes, I take the urn and crouch down so I can safely remove the lid. As I look inside the shiny vessel, something strikes me as odd, the plastic bag inside is open, not the way it was when I got it from the funeral home. I glance at Olivia who immediately diverts my gaze and pretends to focus on her grandmother. For a moment I feel upset at the thought of her going into the urn, but then I realize that Laura didn't just belong to me.

"Do you want to release the ashes?" I ask, motioning the urn toward my daughter.

She shakes her head.

I'm not sure if I should have had a speech prepared or what but for some reason, no words are coming to my mind. My thoughts are in turmoil as I hold onto the open urn. Why did you do what you did, Laura. You were loved, so very loved. I can tell by the look on both my daughter and Greta's face that they are thinking the same thing. And with that, I reach into the vase and slowly begin tipping it until the grains of dust and whisps of silt slowly drift out of the opening and mix with the sea. Once the urn is empty, the three of us watch as the remnants of ashes ebb and flow on the edges of the shore before they expand and are carried out to the deeper waters.

"Are you okay?" I look at Olivia who is staring out at the sparkling sea.

She shrugs. "It doesn't matter if I am or not. She's gone now."

Taking a chance and being rejected, I reach out and put a hand on Greta's shoulder, "What about you, Greta? How are you holding up?"

She looks up at me, her blue eyes mirroring her late daughter's, "She chose her own fate when she left Comox to go to the city. Her life derailed after that."

I quickly remove my hand and bite my tongue. What an ice queen. I can't imagine what Laura endured growing up with this bitter woman.

After a slow walk back to the cabin, Greta stands in front of her car. "Can I keep the urn?" she says, pointing to the bronze container I am holding.

After glancing at Olivia and seeing no signs of objection, I hand the urn to the woman and turn to go inside. My daughter stays outside, speaking with her grandmother, and I feel a wave of relief wash over me. At least my interactions with Greta are done for now. I can only hope that, in the time we have left here, the old witch doesn't add any more negativity to my daughter's already fragile mind.

A while later, Olivia walks in and shuts the door behind her. "I'm going to go to Grandma's and stay the night tonight," she says, then adds, "If that's okay."

She clearly hesitates, thinking twice about telling me rather than asking, especially after her little disappearing act the other night.

"Are you sure that's such a good idea?" I ask, my concern rising. "You've just been through something really emotional. Don't you want to stay here and let things soak in a bit?"

She shakes her head. "No. Not really. I think I'd feel a lot better being around Mom's family and looking at old pictures and stuff."

As much as I want her to stay home, I know I have no right to argue her point.

"Alright," I finally say, "you can go. But make sure you call me if anything gets strange over there."

Then, to my surprise, she lunges toward me. I instinctively raise my arms to stop her, but when she reaches me, her embrace is weak. She wraps her arms around my waist and buries her face in my chest, sobbing. And for that brief moment, she's five years old again, holding me the way she used to when I'd come home from work, running to greet me with the same heartfelt embrace she gave me every time I walked through the door. Suddenly, all my worries about her mental state disappear and I have hope once again that she'll be just fine.

"I love you, kiddo!" I say, sniffing back a tear.

"You too, Dad," she replies before lifting her eyes to meet mine. Seeing her mother's ashes released into the sea did exactly what I hoped it would—it brought her back to me, and more importantly, back to herself. A tear slips down her cheek, and I gently brush it away. She smiles, "I guess I'd better grab my toothbrush and a change of clothes," she says, releasing me from our embrace. "Grandma's waiting in the car."

While Olivia heads to her room, I sink into the sofa, exhaling a deep, almost forgotten breath. It's the first full breath I've taken since Laura died.

A few minutes later, Olivia returns, a small armful of clothes and her toiletries case in hand. "Bye, Dad," she says, fumbling with the doorknob before finally managing to open it. "I'll see you tomorrow."

* * *

The rest of my day passes quietly, allowing me the rare chance to relax and reflect on Laura without being consumed by guilt. I think about the good memories we shared, and for once, the weight on my chest feels a little lighter. As the day slips into night, I walk over to the window, hoping to spot Mary on the beach. Though I barely know her, her kind demeanor has a way of drawing me in, making me want to share the story of scattering Laura's ashes and the breakthrough I had with Olivia afterward. But I can't see any sign of Mary, so I decide to go to bed instead. Maybe tomorrow, when Olivia gets home, we can do something together.

Walking past Olivia's room, I notice her door is ajar and looking inside, I see that her window is still half-open. I smile and grin. I swear, if that kid's head wasn't attached to her body, she'd forget it. As soon as I open her door fully, an icy cold breeze rushes in, sending a shiver down my spine. It's strange, because I don't remember it being this cold when we were outside just hours ago. I quickly cross the room and close her window.

As I turn to head back to the door, a magazine catches my eye, blown onto the floor. I reach down to pick it up, but when I straighten, I notice something else under her bed—a book. Upon closer inspection, I realize it's her journal.

For a brief moment, the thought crosses my mind to open it, to see if she's written anything about that night she snuck out—about who she met and where she went. But after the hug we shared earlier and the moments of closeness, something inside me shifts. I want to let the past go, to start with a clean slate, and that includes learning to trust her again.

I leave the journal untouched, carefully place the magazine on the bed, and leave the room exactly as she left it.

* * *

With the down duvet over me, my pajamas, and socks on, I still can't shake the chill I felt in Olivia's room. I toss and turn, trying to get comfortable, but the cold lingers. Frustrated, I quickly get up and check the thermostat in my room. The needle hasn't budged, still reading the same cozy level it's been at since we arrived. I climb back into bed, wrapping the quilt tightly around me.

As I exhale, a cloud of fog escapes in front of me. This is crazy. Why the hell does it feel so damn cold in here when the thermostat is fine? Maybe the emotional stress I've been under has lowered my resistance and I've picked up something. Either way, it's strange how suddenly it's hit me. It takes me a good hour of shivering until I can relax enough to fade off to sleep.

* * *

The most haunting, blood-curdling screech of a raging woman's voice erupts down the hallway, a sound so powerful and full of fury that it rips me from sleep. My heart slams against my chest, so hard I feel like it's going to explode. I jerk upright, gasping for breath, my body frozen in shock. The scream still echoes in my ears, reverberating through the walls of the house.

I shove the blankets aside and scramble out of bed, my limbs trembling with fear as I rush to the bedroom door. With a shaking hand, I throw it open, my breath coming in short, sharp gasps.

As I look down the hall toward Olivia's room, my gaze is drawn to something impossible—two bright lights, hovering just above the floor. One is a stark, glowing blue, the other a pulsating, deep red. They hover, facing each other in a bizarre standoff, as if locked in some silent, unholy dance.

The icy air is thick around me as foggy vapor escapes my mouth. I stand motionless, unable to tear my eyes away from the strange lights. The silence is suffocating, broken only by the pounding of my own heart and the deafening screech still ringing in my ears. I don't know what I'm seeing, but I know one thing: I shouldn't be here.

Without warning, the swirling colors seemed to sense my gaze, and in a sudden, fluid motion, they twist upward toward the ceiling. For a fleeting, breathless moment, the colors pulse with energy before shooting over my head and disappearing into the wall behind me. I glance up at the ceiling light, which flares so bright that I fear it might explode. After a tense few seconds, the brightness fades back to normal, and warmth slowly returns to the small cabin. My mind is spinning as I go to my room and sit on the edge of the bed, hoping to settle my pounding heart. I honestly cannot explain what just happened. I don't believe in spirits, I never have, but those pulsating masses of light, they weren't manufactured, they were real entities. I could feel their energy, and I know they could feel mine. For some reason, I wasn't afraid of the blue one, but the red one, there was something unholy, something evil about it and although I can't explain what the hell I just saw, I pray I never see it again.

* * *

Even though the cabin is warm again, I'm too uneasy to relax enough to sleep. My mind is exhausted as I try to rationalize the strange orbs. Was I losing my mind? Had the guilt of Laura's death been too much to bear and something finally snapped in my head? Or had I eaten something bad, and got food poisoning? But I know that's not it, otherwise I'd be throwing up and in major stomach pain. To ease my mind and calm my racing thoughts, I decide to go for a walk on the beach and get some air. Once I'm dressed into my street clothes and have put on my shoes and coat, I glance at the clock, it's 2 am, and I step out into the night and close the door.

For some reason, I feel safer out here under the vast clear sky with no walls to confine me. I slowly walk to the shoreline and watch the gentle waves cascade over the sand. My eyes scan the shallows, and I find myself looking for my new friend, Mary's necklace, a good distraction from my thoughts right now. As I strain to see around the small rocks, I hear a noise behind me, considering what I've just went through, I turn around quickly as my pulse quickens. A hooded figure with a small frame is making their way toward me. Not knowing what to expect, I stiffen and push my shoulders back, preparing myself for another weird encounter. But, then, I see two dainty hands raise up and push the hood back revealing Mary's pretty face. I exhale loudly and smile. In a few short moments, she is standing only a few feet in front of me.

"You startled me," I laugh.

"Little old me frightening such a big guy? I doubt that," she smiles.

It's good to see her, well, it's good to see anyone after the night I've had, but especially her.

"What are you doing out so late?" I ask.

"She shrugs. "I had a bad dream. Old ghosts, I guess."

An offhanded comment, one I've heard before but unbeknownst to her, the words are a little too familiar right now.

"What were you looking for as I was walking up?"

I smile, feeling a bit embarrassed. "I wasn't looking for anything, just thought since I was out here I might as well keep my eyes open for that trinket you're missing."

She reached out and puts her hand on mine, "Thank you. I appreciate the help."

Her hands are as cold as ice and I unintentionally jerk mine away. "Wow, girl. You are freezing. You should have gloves on."

She giggles and tells me she's had circulation issues for years and how despite her cold hands, she always feels warm—something I'm not used to hearing from a slender girl. Every other woman I've known who was thin always seemed to get the chills, even Laura. Though she was fit, there wasn't much meat on her bones, and she'd often ask me to close the windows and turn up the heat in the house. "Now we're both here, should we take a little stroll?" she asks.

I walk beside her as we slowly make our way up the beach, keeping our eyes on the shallows for her necklace.

"You seem a bit uneasy. Is everything okay?" Mary says, stopping.

Taken aback, I stop and look at her. "Uneasy? I didn't think I was acting uneasy."

She grins sympathetically then resumes walking. "It's none of my business, really. I was just making an observation."

I don't want her to feel threatened by me especially since being out here with her is helping distract me from thinking about the strange incident that happened in the cabin.

Trying to appear more relaxed, I take a breath and then tell her that I've had a stressful evening but I am feeling a lot better now that I'm outside in the fresh air.

Again, she stops walking, this time she makes eye contact, "Well, since we both can't sleep, maybe telling me your troubles will help. It's worth a shot, right?"

In normal circumstances, I would never divulge my problems to someone I barely know, but the truth is I really do need someone to talk to. However, suspecting she would probably run fast in the other direction if I told her about the weird orb things in the cabin that miraculously floated in the hallway and then disappeared into the walls, I opt to keep that part out of the conversation.

As we walk slowly along the waters edge, I feel a sense of peace come over me. Mary seems sweet and even though she's practically a stranger, something makes me trust her. It doesn't take long before I'm diving into the reason I'm in the Valley, my wife Laura who was so lonely because I spent all of my time working to give her a good life, that she sought affection from another man then after her affair, she couldn't live with the guilt so she jumped from our penthouse apartment and ended her suffering. I went on to explain how my daughter has been distant and mean, until recently. Then, I mention how I found Olivia's journal and the strange pictures and writings I saw. Much to my surprise, Mary doesn't comment on the tragedy of my wife committing suicide or her affair, instead, she focuses on Olivia's journal and wants to know what kind of drawings I saw and what she had written regarding witchcraft.

I dismiss the reasoning for this as a maternal presence that is in most women. Maybe Mary thinks that there's no reason to discuss Laura or what happened because she's dead, but Olivia, a young girl, is showing signs of emotional distress, a call for help. I respond by trying to remember the parts in the journal where I saw symbols, what they looked like and the spells and words I read while Mary listened intently. Once I was finished talking, Mary thought for a few minutes, her brows furrowed and her lips pierced, "Could you show me the book sometime? I think I may be able to help her, through you of course, I wouldn't want to speak to her directly, especially since if I did, she would know that you were in her private diary and then to make things even worse, you told me, a total stranger about it."

I pause for a moment, feeling confused. My first impulse is to ask her about her training with troubled teenagers, but I hesitate—I don't want to challenge her, especially since she's only trying to help. Instead, I ask, "Are you sure you want to see the book? Olivia will be home sometime tomorrow, and I'm not sure if I'll have a chance to grab it. I don't know if she'll be staying at her grandma's again before we have to leave."

Mary places her hand on mine, but this time I don't flinch from her icy cold skin. "I think if I could read what she wrote, it might give me some insight into where her thoughts are—whether she's in a bad place, or if it's just a young girl trying to make sense of the tragedy of losing her mother in such a horrible way. If you're not sure you'll have another chance after tonight, we could go to your cabin while we're both still awake and unable to sleep, and I could take a look now."

I'm taken aback by her suggestion, especially that she'd want to come to the cabin alone with me—someone she's only just met. "Are you sure?" I ask. She nods with confidence.

Considering I don't have anyone else showing any interest in helping, I agree. "I guess it couldn't hurt. Olivia will never know, so... yeah, we could do that."

* * *

A wave of guilt hits me as I realize I'm revealing my daughter's innermost thoughts to someone she's never met. Reluctantly, I fetch Olivia's journal from under her bed and head back to the living room, where Mary is waiting. She takes the book from me with a gentle nod, then walks over to the couch and sits down. As she slowly flips through the pages, I offer her a drink. Without looking up, she shakes her head.

I, on the other hand, could use one, so I pour myself a shot of scotch and sit in a chair while Mary reads. Every so often, I try to gauge her expression, wondering if anything in the journal is shocking her, but so far, she remains stone-faced, deeply focused on the pages.

Finally, with my drink finished and my eyes getting heavy, Mary closes the book, making a noise that alerts me and causes me to sit up straight.

"Well, was there anything too troubling in there or…"

Mary takes a long breath then with a seriousness meets my gaze. "I think your daughter may have stumbled on something she knows nothing about—something dangerous.

"What do you mean by dangerous?" I say, wondering what I could've missed when I skimmed through the pages a few nights ago.

"I think Olivia needs special help."

"Like from a psychiatrist, you mean?"

She scoffs, "No. They can't help her."

"Then, who?" I ask, starting to feel concern.

"I can try to help her." Mary shrugs.

Not wanting to insult her, I gently approach the subject of psychologists and ask her if she's had training in the field. She tells me that she has had a far more valuable learning in the field, personal experience.

"I'm not really sure if my daughter will open up to you. When her mother died, I took her to get counselling but it was futile, after just a couple of sessions I was told that Olivia was a closed book and that I was just wasting my money until she was ready to talk about er feelings."

Mary giggles, "I've never had much use for professionals in that field. I've never been to one and I don't plan on going either. My approach would be to try and undo the damage that she has brought on herself."

Brought on herself? What a strange thing to say. How can a child of Olivia's age have brought on her own grief? I'm just about to ask her when Mary stands up and walks out into the hallway. "Tell me, have you seen anything strange happen in this house?"

Her question causes the air to suddenly escape my lungs, as if I've been hit in the gut.

"Strange like how?" I ask, unsure if I want to tell her about the strange moving lights and the screeching I heard. As strange as her question sounds, maybe she's referring to something simple and I don't want to come off like a freak.

Mary turns and faces me then after a quick moment, she grins, "Never mind. I should probably get going, the sun will be up soon and I'm sure you could use some rest."

I nod, "Yeah. It has been a long night for sure."

I walk with Mary to the door and hold it open as she steps out into the night. She turns to face me, saying she'll be on the beach tomorrow night, but much earlier—around 10 p.m. "If you come out, it's important that you bring your daughter so we can meet."

"I nod. I just hope she doesn't go ballistic when she finds out both you and I have read her journal."

Mary presses a finger to her lips. "I won't say a word."

Once she disappears into the shadows, I close the door, then walk over to the couch and sit down. Her question about whether I've seen anything unusual in the cabin have me confused. What did she mean? I replay the strange incident that happened when I was alone—the blue and red lights, hovering and alive with an incredible energy, one good and one evil. But it can't be. I'm a logical person, always have been. I've never believed in ghosts or the boogeyman, not even as a child. Still, something happened here that defies reason—something my logical mind can't begin to explain.

Chapter Seven

After a restless night, I manage to get a few hours of sleep once the sun comes up. It's humbling to admit to myself that I was afraid, but I was. Every time a tree branch scraped against the windows or the wind howled around the cabin, my hands would tremble. I even considered sleeping in the car, but I knew Olivia would be dropped off by her grandmother, and I didn't want to be caught napping outside in the vehicle .

I take a long shower to wake myself up, followed by a strong cup of coffee. After getting dressed, I text Olivia. Thankfully, she still sounds as approachable as she did before she left. She tells me they're almost at the house, then hangs up. A few moments later, she walks through the door with an armful of small boxes.

"What do you have there?" I ask.

"Pictures of Mom when she was young. Grandma said I could keep them." She heads down the hall to her room, smiling happily as she clutches her treasures.

For a second, panic sets in, and I wonder if I placed her journal back exactly as I found it under her bed. But when she reappears and I see that she doesn't look angry, I exhale in relief.

"Dad, I didn't feel like having breakfast this morning, but I'm kind of hungry now. Can we go out to eat?"

My first instinct is to tell her we have food here, but after her positive attitude shift since we scattered Laura's ashes, I don't want to do anything to bring her back to that dark place, especially not with me. "Sure, I say. Let me get my coat and shoes on."

As we drive up Comox Avenue, Olivia turns on the radio. When a song from the

'80s starts playing, she taps her hand on her knee in rhythm with the music. I haven't seen her act like a normal teenager in so long. I just hope this means that she's finally dealing with her mother's death.

* * *

Once again the food at Tidal Café in Comox is excellent and we enjoy our breakfast. When we're done, Olivia grabs a local paper and spots an ad for a gallery in Courtenay. "Can we check it out after we leave here?" she asks.

I nod then motion for the waitress to bring us our bill. Once I settle up for the meal, we head for Courtenay.

After Olivia finally gets the directions right, we arrive at Artful-The Gallery and step out of the car. The moment we walk through the doors, I am struck by the vibrant, colorful paintings lining the walls of the beautifully curated space. The room has an easy, calming energy, with cozy couches and chairs placed just right, almost inviting you to slow down, take a seat, and really absorb what's around you.

Olivia is drawn to a painting of water—deep blues and soft whites, rippling across the canvas. It reminds me of the place where we scattered Laura's ashes, and I can see by the way Olivia is looking at it that she's thinking the same thing. We spend an hour wandering through the gallery, taking it all in, but Olivia keeps circling back to that one painting. Eventually, she stands in front of it and turning to me with a pleading look in her eyes, she says "Dad, I just have to have this picture. It reminds me of where we scattered Mom's ashes."

It's not exactly a budget-friendly purchase, but the way she's looking at it—like it holds a piece of something she doesn't want to let go of—I don't hesitate. I pull out my credit card and pay for the artwork, happy to give her something that clearly means so much.

Once we've carefully loaded the painting into the car, Olivia turns to me with a grateful smile. "Thanks, Dad," she says. "I'm going to hang it in my room when we get back to the penthouse in Vancouver."

But soon her expression falters, and she looks at me seriously. "Are we going to keep living in the penthouse, Dad?"

The truth is, I don't really know how to answer her. We uprooted her from our house in Shaunessy to move to the penthouse downtown after Laura confessed that she had an affair. She thought that by moving we could start over and forget about what she did—but of course we couldn't. Right after she decided to take her life, we had to stay at a downtown hotel while the police and investigators conducted their investigations. It was only the past few weeks that we were able to return. I think that Olivia doesn't want to move from the penthouse because it's the last place she saw her mom. I get that. But what my daughter isn't considering is that everyone in the building who knows we live on the top floor will be whispering as we walk by, Oh there goes the poor husband and daughter of the woman who killed herself. And I'm not prepared to put myself or Olivia through that. Still, I don't want Olivia to feel sad so, I simply tell her that I'm not sure if we'll be staying in the penthouse permanently.

* * *

Once Olivia has a shower and does her hair—a two-hour ordeal, she comes out of her room wearing her black hoodie and black pants. "Dad. I was thinking maybe we could go to Courtenay and check out some of the clothing stores. I'm kinda tired of wearing black."

Thank God! "That's a great idea," I respond enthusiastically, hoping that this is

91

another sign of her coming out of her dark stage.

After we lock the door and get into the car, she suggests that if I'm up for it, maybe we could catch a movie after shopping. I smile and agree, grateful for the sudden change in her attitude toward me. I knew that spreading her mother's ashes would have some impact on her, closure to some degree. I just never dreamt she would progress this quickly.

Courtenay is about a quarter of the size of one of the small cities in the Fraser Valley, like Abbotsford or Chilliwack, but the people here seem more down-to-earth which is refreshing. On the mainland, people stick to themselves and although they are mostly pleasant, they're not very personable.

We drive up 5th Street where a strip of quaint shops line both sides of the narrow road. Olivia points at a stylish storefront as we roll by, West Coast Karma. "There, Dad. I want to go in there."

I find a place to park and we get out of the car and I walk over to her on the sidewalk.

"Dad, be serious. Please tell me you're not coming to try on clothes with me. I would just die!"

I grin, "Teenagers!"

I reach into my wallet and slide out one of my credit cards then hand it to her, "Don't go too crazy."

She laughs, "Don't worry. This isn't Robson Street in Vancouver. There's no Aritzia around here."

I spot a one-level building with the words Courtenay Library on a sign in front and tell Olivia to find me in there once she's finished abusing my credit card. She grins, then waves her hand and heads for the shop.

* * *

Inside the library I'm struck by how different this one is to the libraries I've visited back home. People smile at me as I walk past, and there are two ladies at the check-out counter who immediately offer their help in finding anything I'd like to rad. I ask about books on the history of the Comox Valley thinking that Olivia may be interested in knowing more about the area where her mother grew up. They help me choose a few books on the background of the Valley, complete with black and white pictures, and I'm just about to sign those out when another title catches my eye, The dark Past of The Comox Valley. I pick up the book and sit at a nearby table to sift through the pages. With each page I turn I discover fascinating stories that seem to jump off the page. The infamous, Flying Dutchman who was Henry Wagner, the last man hanged in 1914 on the Island. Wagner was an infamous criminal who wreaked havoc up and down the coast until getting cornered in Union Bay, not far from here. During the same time there were, mining strikes that left many people starving and living in shanty's or tents while they protested. The book seemed full of unusual glimpses into the past. Near the back of the book is a chapter on Haunted structures and ghosts. I laugh to myself and then slowly scan the pages. Old house restaurant where Lena, a young woman lived as a nanny in the early 1900's who drowned mysteriously on evening in a river beside the building. Sandwick Manor, Aunt Anna, a woman who lived with her husband in 1911, The last entry is about an Indigenous woman who married a European settler in Comox during the mid 1800s. She was said to be of remarkable beauty and good character but she disappeared and it was rumoured that her jealous husband murdered her, but no charges were ever brought against him because her body was never found. I'm just about to read more on the story when Olivia walks up with a bag over her shoulder and a smile on her face. "I had fun shopping, dad. I found a few new tops, not black ones, she laughs. I wish they had a West Coast Karma store on the mainland. I didn't know what to expect when I walked in, this is a small town after all, but everything they had was trendy and it wasn't even that expensive." She passes me my credit card.

I close the book and walk up to the counter and sign out the three books. Once we're back in the car, Olivia searches where the movie theatres are on her phone. "Dad. I can't believe the Wolf Man movie is playing here. I've wanted to see it for months. Can we go?" she asks eagerly.

"Wolf Man? I have to sit through two hours of a movie that's called Wolf Man?" I say. shaking my head.

"Yes. But they probably have a ton of really yummy greasy snacks there that we can stuff our faces with."

"Oh great, I'll get to poison my mind and my body at the same time."

With hours to kill before the show starts, we tour around Courtenay and check out a few fun little stores while taking in the local culture. Everyone is polite and welcoming which makes the rest of the day pass quickly. Once it's time to go to the show, we drive down Cliff Avenue to The Driftwood Mall and find a parking spot near the modest theatre.

* * *

Surrounded by a few dozen screaming teens and their reluctant parents, my ears are ringing by the time the show finally ends. The kind of entertainment these kids crave today amazes me—blood, gore, and almost no plot. Olivia can't stop raving about the movie on the way home, and I'm instantly reminded of the generation gap between us. By the time we return to the cabin and get into our pajamas, I'm ready for bed.

Olivia says good night and heads to her room, and I walk over to the front window and gaze out at the calm sea. Despite the hack-and-slash movie I had to endure, today has been a great one. For the first time in months, I feel hopeful about the future. I'm just about to turn off the living room lamp when out of my peripheral view I see a slender figure on the beach—Mary.

Then I remember —I was supposed to bring Olivia to meet Mary so the two of them could talk. Mary seemed determined to help Olivia with the disturbing things she'd seen in her journal. But honestly, I believe whatever stress led Olivia to write those dark entries is behind her now. She's as happy and normal as I could hope for, and I don't want anyone making her revisit that morbid place.

I turn off the lamp and head to bed, hoping Mary won't be upset until I can explain that Olivia's outlook has improved, and that she's not the same girl she was when she wrote those journal entries.

Chapter Eight

It's three in the morning when a bloodcurdling scream rips through the silence of the cabin, coming from Olivia's room. Disoriented and panicked, I sprint down the hall and burst into her room to find her huddled in the corner, knees drawn to her chest, her phone clutched tightly in her trembling hands. She's shaking uncontrollably and her eyes are wide with terror.

"What happened?" I ask, rushing to her side. Her skin feels ice-cold to the touch.

"Something tried to get me, Dad. It was so horrible," she gasps, her voice panicked with fear.

I help her to her feet, pulling her tightly into my arms. "Do you want to go back to bed?"

She shakes her head vigorously. "No. Please... get me out of here. I want to go to your room with you. I don't want to be alone," she sobs, clinging to me for life.

As I take her hand and walk her toward my room, I can't help but wonder what kind of nightmare could've caused this kind of reaction. This isn't like the nightmares she used to have, the ones that would send her crawling into Laura's and my bed for comfort. Her fear feels different, deeper, more real.

Once we reach my bed, Olivia crawls over the mattress and picks up one of my pillows and cradles it in front of her. "It was so scary dad. I really thought it was going to kill me or take me away." She says, starting to slowly rock.

I walk over and sit next to her on the bed. "Do you want to tell me what happened?"

She shakes her head, "Not really but I think I have to, otherwise it will stay in my head."

"Take your time," I say, stroking her back.

I was lying in my bed and just about to go to sleep when I heard this horrible screeching noise. It sounded like it was coming from the wall across from my bed. So, I sat up and listened really closely and then all of a sudden, I saw a glowing red spot on the wall and it just kept getting bigger."

Red glowing light? How could she have seen the same thing I did. This is surreal and very troubling. But I need to let her finish telling me what happened.

"Then, I tried to move but I was frozen in place. And when I opened my mouth to yell for you, no noise came out." More tears flowed down her pale cheeks.

"And that's when I saw it. That's when the demon thing sprang out of the wall and zoomed over my bed and suspended itself over me. It's eyes were hideous dad. And when it lowered itself over my body, it opened its mouth and I saw fire in its throat. It was so angry, it hated me. It dropped down like it meant to flatten itself over my body, then it hung there for a few minutes, before it kind of shoved me into the mattress and then it flew into the wall and disappeared."

She turns her face to mine, locking eyes with me. "If you believe anything I've ever told you, believe this. And I wasn't dreaming it—I was wide awake."

I try to gather my thoughts, but I can't find the right words. I look down at my feet.

"I can tell you don't believe me," she says, her voice trembling. "You think it was just a nightmare, don't you?"

I slowly shake my head, not wanting to share my own experience with the strange pulsating lights. If I tell her, she'll know for sure that whatever is haunting us is real. Parents are supposed to protect their kids from fear, to tell them that things like the boogeyman don't exist.

I take a breath and answer carefully. "Of course I believe you, Olivia. I just... I'm not sure what you saw, that's all."

She seems to relax a bit at my response, settling back onto her side, still clutching the pillow. "I'll be right back," I tell her, then head to the kitchen to warm some milk.

When I return, I set the milk on the nightstand beside her and grab my laptop from my side of the bed. As I search online for lighthearted stories to distract her from the terrifying experience she just had, Olivia sniffles and wipes her eyes.

I find a light-heated short story and begin reading aloud while she sips the warm milk.

"I feel like a little kid again," she says, managing a weak smile. "Like when you and Mom would let me sleep with you when I was scared. Mom would make me a cup of warm milk, and you'd read to me from one of my storybooks."

I reach out and gently rub the top of her head. "Try to lay back and relax your mind."

Before long, Olivia is asleep, her hand still wrapped tightly around my arm. With my free hand, I move my laptop onto the nightstand and lie back on the pillow. I think about what Olivia saw in her room. If it weren't for my own experience with the strange glowing lights, I might just chalk her claims up to hormones or an anxiety attack, but neither of those explanations seem to fit. The truth is, there's something here—and whatever it is, it's angry.

Maybe tomorrow I'll look into finding a new place to stay, but I'll wait until I can gauge Olivia's state of mind in the morning. With her hand still clutching my arm, I drift off to sleep.

Suddenly, a loud banging on the front door jolts me awake. Olivia screams, her fear now palpable. I try to calm her, not wanting her to become hysterical. "It's okay. It's probably just someone at the wrong address. Stay here, I'll be right back," I say, reassuringly.

Olivia sniffles, her voice shaky. "Be careful."

As I make my way down the hall, I wonder if the person knocking could be Mary. I don't know anyone else in the area, especially not someone who would be up at this hour. When I reach the door, I peer through the window and see a portly figure, but it's too dark to make out any features.

"Who is it?" I call, raising my voice.

"Who do you think it is, dingbat? Santa Claus?" The broken English and the insult immediately give her away. It's Greta, but what on earth is she doing here at this hour?

I open the door to find the old woman standing in her robe, her hair wrapped tightly in curlers. "What are you doing here so late?" I ask, still trying to make sense of her unexpected appearance.

"Well, I didn't come here for my health, did I? And why did it take you so long to let me in? I'm old, you could've made me freeze to death out here!" She pushes past me without waiting for an invitation. "Now, where is my granddaughter?"

I hear Olivia holler from my room, "I'm here grandma." Then, she runs down the hall and wraps her arms around Greta while looking up at me. "I called her, Dad. When I was in my bed and too scared to move."

"Olivia, you had no right to call anyone so late."

Greta shoots me a glare through squinting eyes, "I am not anyone! I am her family." Greta motions for Olivia to sit on the couch and then joins her. "Now, child. Tell me about your nightmare."

"It wasn't a nightmare, grandma. I saw something evil. It was in my room and it was trying to hurt me."

Greta smiles and then gently strokes Olivia's hair, "No. No, honey. There is no such thing that can hurt you. Maybe you ate some food that didn't agree with you and it caused you to have such a nightmare."

Olivia groans and covers her face with her hands. "I didn't have a nightmare, grandma. I really saw something and it was awful."

Greta looks up at me. "I am not sure what is going on here but this child is very upset. I think it's best that she comes home with me."

I want to tell her that Olivia is going to be fine and she should mind her own business but seeing the state my daughter is in, I concede to the fact that she is probably better off spending the night with her grandmother. Even though Olivia is upset that her grandmother dismissed her claims that she did see something terrible, she agrees to leave with Greta, probably because she's too afraid to stay here and risk another ghostly encounter. I can't say I blame her and after Olivia gathers a bag with a change of clothes, she and Greta headed out.

* * *

Some Like it Hot and The Odd Couple, two shows I used to watch with my dad on a regular basis, helped distract me through the night. I'm so glad I packed my laptop for this trip.

Every so often, I'd hear a screeching noise from the front room. After checking it out, I realize it's just tree branches scraping against the windows. I didn't see any more pulsing blue and red lights, but my mind wouldn't let me calm down so sleep was impossible.

Finally, a glance at the clock on the bedside table displayed 8 AM. Time to get moving. A quick shower to shake off the grogginess and then it's time to try and figure out whatever the hell Olivia and I saw here in the cabin.

Once I'm dressed and feeling a little more human, I head to the kitchen for coffee—extra strong this morning—and a couple slices of toast. Sitting on the couch, sipping my coffee, I stare out to sea and wonder if Mary was out on the shore last night, looking for her necklace. Did she wait for me to join her? Is she upset that I didn't bring Olivia to meet her. Would she have an explanation for what happened to us last night?

Chapter Nine

An angry downpour obstructs my vision and causes me to drive at a snail's pace down the Dyke Road toward Courtenay. Once I navigate my way over a small bridge and head West on 6th Street, I pull up in front of a quaint old church with a pointed roof. Sitting in my car, staring at the white building, I snicker to myself. I can't believe I'm actually considering going inside a church to try and find answers to the strange orbs I saw last night. But Olivia's terrifying experience has me desperate. I'm not remotely religious. I don't know the bible and after meeting Greta years ago, a hugely religious person, I decided that if churches had people like her in their congregations, I wanted no part of them. Besides my wife was raised in the church, and she wanted nothing to do with organized religion. I am spiritual, which in my mind means that I believe in God, as did Laura. So, the fact that I'm here and considering gong inside a church, is something I never dreamt I'd be doing. That being said, I don't know where else to turn for advice, or maybe for someone to give me a simple explanation to what I saw. I take a deep breath as I turn off the ignition then stuff the keys in my jacket pocket. I guess if I meet the pastor and he thinks I'm nuts after I tell him my story, at least I don't live around here so I'll never have to see him again.

I step out of the car and make my way up the narrow cement path to the tall wooden doors. Gripping the iron handle, I pull them open and step inside. There are three rows of pews stretching across the small church's floor. The windows, stained in vibrant colors, bathe the room in light, a striking contrast to the nasty weather outside. At the far end of the center aisle stands a stage, with a wooden podium at its center. Behind it, a door bears the word "Office" engraved in black. My footsteps echo on the wooden floors as I make my way toward the office door. *What am I doing?* I ask myself. I must be out of my mind. But back at the cabin, all I could think about was finding the answers to what Olivia and I had seen. I can't go to the cops—they'd probably detain me, make me take a breathalyzer. A church was the only approachable place that came to mind.

I'm just about to rap on the door when I lose my nerve and turn to leave, but the door opens behind me.

"Can I help you?" a soft male voice asks.

I turn to see a rather short man with light-hair who has a gym body and is wearing modern style clothes—not at all what I expected.

I grin awkwardly. "Hi. I umm. I was looking for some answers or umm advice. But, I changed my mind." I say, hoping that he lets me go without asking anymore questions. But no such luck.

"What kind of questions do you have?" he asks, motioning toward a bench in front of the church.

I sigh and take a seat with him sitting beside me.

"Is there something on your mind?"

I shrug, feeling uncomfortable under the pressure. "I'd rather not say. It's something really strange, and if I tell you, you'll probably think I'm crazy." I let out a small scoff. "If my daughter hadn't seen the same thing, I'd think I was crazy too."

The pastor chuckles. "Believe me, there's nothing you could say that would surprise me. I've heard it all."

For the first time, I notice his eyes—a warm, golden brown that somehow make me feel like I can trust him.

"My name's Paul," he says, extending his hand.

I shake it, exhaling a bit more steadily. "I'm Oliver. Nice to meet you."

"A moment ago, you mentioned seeing something. Why don't you tell me about it?"

Slowly, I explain that I'm visiting the Valley with my daughter and that we came here to release my wife's ashes. Then, I tell him how I fell asleep and was awoken to the blood-curdling screeches in the cabin and how when I got out of bed to investigate, I saw the strange lights in the hallway. And then went on to reiterate that the very next night my daughter was awakened by the one of the strange glowing lights in her room, only this light morphed into some kind of demonic being and her experience was a lot more terrifying than mine."

"How so?" Paul asks, looking surprisingly unfazed.

"The red glowing thing my daughter saw manifested into some sort of beast and it terrorized her before hovering over her, almost like it planned to enter her body, and then suddenly disappearing into the wall. She was hysterical and more frightened than I have ever seen her."

Paul takes a moment and seems to be thinking as his gaze drops to the floor.

"It's a hard one to answer, if that's what you're looking for." He says, resuming eye contact. "I've heard many stories of ghost or spirit sightings, some good, some bad. Most of the time my advice to people is to find protection and solace with prayer and reading the bible. Do you have a relationship with God?"

I explain apologetically that although I do believe in God, I do not go to church nor have I read the bible.

Paul smiles, "If you believe in Christ and have your own relationship with him, you are a Christian, regardless of if you belong to a church or not."

He's definitely a non-judgement type, which I like. I should introduce Greta to him so s he can see what a true Christian should act like.

"About the sightings that you and your daughter experienced, and I do believe that you both saw something, otherwise you wouldn't be here. I can tell you that some Christians believe that what appear to be ghosts could be souls in purgatory, evil spirits."

I feel my eyes widen, "Wow. That doesn't sound comforting. So, let's say that what we saw were in fact ghosts, how do we get them to go away?" I hear the words as they leave my lips and I cringe with how ridiculous I sound. I can't believe I'm talking about ghosts.

Paul leans in and puts a hand on my shoulder. "As much as you feel alone in what you're going through, you're not. If your unwanted visitors return, I invite you to come back here. We have members of the congregation and me that will come to the cabin and hold a prayer group."

I nod slowly and thank him for the offer. At least now if the demons come back we have somewhere to turn for help.

* * *

As I drive back to Comox, the rain eases and I see the most stunning rainbow in the distance. Even though Paul didn't offer an immediate explanation to what the orbs at the cabin could be, at least he didn't make a fool of me for telling him my crazy story.

As I pull up to the cabin, I notice Olivia sitting on the front step with her bag resting against her legs. I wasn't expecting her this early in the day. Unless she's going to school, she normally sleeps until late morning or early afternoon.

"You're here. I thought you'd still be sleeping."

Olivia shakes her head solemnly. "No. I actually couldn't sleep last night so I waited until Grandma got up and I asked her to take me home."

Figuring that her insomnia is due to the scary phenomenon she saw in her room, I don't question her, instead, I unlock the door and put my arm around her and walk her inside.

I ask her if she'd like to lay down on my bed as I'm pretty sure she doesn't want to go anywhere near her room yet. She tells me that she has something to tell me then walks over and slumps down on the couch. I pour us each a glass of water then walk over and sit down beside her.

"I've done something really bad, Dad. You're probably going to be really angry when I tell you."

"What trouble could you have possibly gotten into at your grandmas?" I smile reassuringly. I'm sure whatever you're going to tell me won't be that bad."

Olivia raises her eyes to meet mine and a lone tear trickles down her cheek. She draws in an audible breath then slowly exhales. "I didn't do anything at grandmas, I did it when I snuck out the other night."

A rush of anxiety rises through my core. Silently, I am praying that she didn't hook up with a boy or something of that magnitude that I am equally unprepared for. "Okay. I'm listening," I say. Unsure if I really want her to know what she did.

Another tear streams down her cheek. "Do you remember when I asked if I could go out and meet some local kids that I met online?"

I nod while keeping her gaze.

"Olivia fidgets with her hands, "Well, I went to meet them that night. I walked up to the store on the corner and they pulled up in a car. There were two girls and two boys."

"Were they the same kind of kids we saw at the mall, the ones wearing all black with face piercings all over?"

She nods. "Yeah. I searched Teen hang outs in the Comox Valley on Facebook and that's how I found them."

Oh no. Is hangouts a new term that means getting together for group sex? A lump forms in my throat.

"Okay. And where did you go with them?"

"We drove up a hill and up to a very old graveyard with a small creepy church on it."

"And?" I force myself to swallow.
More tears fall from Olivia's eyes. "Then, we all walked over to the stone steps of the church and one of the girls pulled a book and some candles out of her purse. And the other girl that was there had a piece of chalk and she drew a big star kind of symbol on the stone." She sniffs and tears continue to fall, then she says, "before I tell you the rest of what happened, I need to tell you about what I've been up to for about the last month."

Pages with strange symbols and dark words from her journal immediately flash through my mind. I almost tell her that I know what she's been writing about but I don't want her to get angry and close the line of communication with me, plus, I need to hear about what she and her new friends did that night.

Olivia continues talking and tells me about dark arts and how she was desperate to conjure up the spirit of her mother so she could ask her why she committed suicide and left us. Now, she's crying so hard, I get up and walk to the bathroom to get her a roll of toilet paper and then return to my spot beside her on the couch.

"Go on," I urge, passing her the tissue.

"Well, that's kind of why I went with those kids that night. While I was talking to them online, they mentioned they were into witchcraft and that's what made me want to meet up. I thought they could help me to speak to mom." She wipes her nose on a wadded-up bunch of paper. "I'm sorry, Dad. I know you must think I'm a freak."

"You're not a freak. You lost your mother and you've been grieving. Grief can make us do strange things."

She forces a smile. "I'm just so mad at her. And I want to know why she would take her own life when I still needed her so much."

Sitting here with my child and looking into her pained face, emotions bubble up in me and before I know it, I too am wiping away tears.

"And there's something else," she says shifting her gaze to the floor. "I took some of moms ashes from the urn."

"Why?" I ask?

She shrugs. "I read in a book that you need ashes or something personal that belong to the dead person you are trying to communicate with."

She says the words so easily, as if the subject of conjuring the dead is a normal thing and it's at this point that I feel like we've reached an impasse. I can either feed into it and not say a word or I can tell her how I really feel about witchcraft. I remind myself that I am not her friend, I am her parent and my job is to do everything I can to keep her on the right path while she's young enough for me to have an influence.

I touch her shoulder and speak softly. "Olivia. I know you were desperate to connect with your mom again. I get that. But there are no such thing as spirits and all of that witchcraft stuff you've been doing is a bunch of bs."

She gasps as she makes eye contact. "I knew you wouldn't believe me!" her voice on the verge of anger.

"I believe that you believe it. I have no doubt about that. But I don't want you to go down a dark rabbit hole and get lost. I want you to be logical and see things as they are in reality."

Olivia shakes her head slowly in disgust. "We were getting close again. And now you say something that makes me feel 100 miles away from you." Her eyes fill with water.

"Don't think of it that way. I'm your dad and it's my responsibility to..."

"You make no sense," she snaps. "Didn't you tell me that you saw the weird floating lights too?"

I'm instantly at a loss for words. She's right. I did tell her what I saw. At this moment, I wish I hadn't. It's not helping my case.

"Well?" she says, expecting and answer.

"I...I don't know, Olivia. Yes, I did see something, something I can't quite explain, but..."

"But, I saw it too. Whatever is here, showed itself to me too, Dad. And honestly, I think I may be the reason it's happening."

I shake my head, "That's ridiculous. Black magic or whatever you think you were doing isn't real."

Olivia raises her voice in frustration. "Then tell me why we never saw anything until after I snuck out and went to the graveyard and did that séance with those kids."

"I don't know. I just don't know. But I can tell you that I mean to get to the bottom of whatever we saw. The important thing is that whatever it was isn't here now. I stayed here alone last night and didn't see a thing."

Olivia seems to relax at this. "So, do you think we'll see whatever or whoever it was again?"

Even though I don't know the answer, I shake my head reassuringly, "I don't. I think we're okay now."

She smiles then leans over and puts her arms around my neck, "I hope you're right."

* * *

TV shows and podcasts often feature hot sauce challenges, a fad that wasn't even on our radar when I was Olivia's age. But in an effort to keep her focused on something more lighthearted and steer her away from thoughts of ghosts and evil spirits, I hesitate but ultimately agree when she challenges me to a hot sauce contest while we're out.

Once we're seated in Tidal Café', Olivia asks the waitress for whatever hot sauces they carry. The woman tilts her head in wonderment which isn't surprising considering neither of us have ordered food yet. I quickly explain and the woman chuckles before taking our order. Olivia opts for Tidal bowl, and I order the smoke brisket, neither one of these dishes seem a good option for a hot sauce challenge. While waiting, Olivia plays on her phone while I look out at the scenery and view the beautiful views of the inlet and the mountains in the background. Once our food arrives, the server sets down our plates then leaves and returns with a few bottles of the liquid fire. Olivia smiles and thanks the woman then looks at me mischievously. "Are ya ready?"

I can feel tightening in my gut already and as my daughter takes the lids off of the small bottles, I have a premonition of sitting on the toilet and groaning in pain. I look down at my plate of food and wish I'd never agreed to the challenge.

"I'll go first," Olivia says.

"Be my guest."

After three good shakes of a red bottle that has what looks to be a devils face on the label, Olivia grabs her fork and stabs her food then stuffs it into her mouth. She stares at me while she chews until her face starts to turn a tinge of red. Once her mouth is empty, she reaches for her water and takes a large swill. "Nothin to it." She lies.

I sigh then grab one of the hot sauce bottles and read the label, Tidal Café' Hot Sauce. I glance over at the waitress who is watching us as she sets a table. I turn the label so she can see my choice and she discreetly gives me a thumbs up. I'm not sure if her gesture is a warning or a sign for, you'll live through it. Hesitantly, I match the amount of hot sauce Olivia used and pour it over my brisket. What a waste. After putting the smallest amount of sauce covered food on my fork, I look at Olivia as I move it into my mouth. The first taste is unexpected. My mouth isn't on fire and the sauce compliments the meat quite nicely. I take another forkful as Olivia looks on, anticipating a dramatic reaction from me. As I chew the next bite, I see my daughters face drop with disappointment. So, I decide to give her what she wants. I widen my eyes and cover my mouth and groan. "Oh, it just hit me. Too hot! Too hot!" I say then reach for my water and drink the entire glass in one long gulp. Olivia cackles. "I win. I win."

I look over at the waitress and wink. She smiles back knowing the game I played.

Thankfully the game is over and I don't have to taste the same liquid fire from the bottle Olivia tasted.

"So, what are we doing after we're finished eating?" she asks.

"I thought we'd take a walk down Comox Ave again, maybe check out a book store or something?"

She shrugs and fakes enthusiasm, "Okay. There's probably not too much to do this early anyway."

When the waitress brings the bill, I leave a very generous tip as a thank you for giving me the thumbs up on the hot sauce . That waitress saved me from suffering with twisting guts the rest of the day.

* * *

Strolling down Comox Avenue, we spend time window shopping, both of us admiring the charming boutiques and shops that line the street. When we reach Island Affair Giftware, the window display, filled with intriguing items, catches our attention.

Olivia and I exchange glances, indicating that we both would like to see what's inside. The moment we enter, we're greeted by the pleasant aroma of soaps and candles. A cheerful lady approaches with a welcoming smile and introduces herself as Lila. After a brief chat, we learn that she showcases art from over 150 local artists.

We continue exploring the shop, which is brimming with unique finds—artistic ornaments, whimsical trinkets, and various treasures strategically placed on the shelves. Olivia wanders off to explore on her own, while I scan the room and find myself drawn to a shelf displaying a small collection of hand-decorated journals.

As I continue exploring the shop, Olivia tells me she's going to run across the street to a bookstore. After about ten minutes, she returns with an excited look on her face and a hardcover book in her hand. "Dad. You are NOT going to believe what I found at the bookstore." She says, passing me the book. "Read the back!"

Curious as to what has her so excited, I read the synopsis on the back cover which talks about how dogs supposedly have special abilities that can predict coming tragedies because they are enlightened to not only this realm but the spirit realm as well. The word spirit makes me thumb through to the middle of the book. As I scan the pages, I read the author's claims that dogs have been used as seers and sentinels because of their ability to detect ghosts, good or evil. And they've even been known to protect their masters when threatened by an evil spirit. Interesting. Probably bullshit, but interesting, nonetheless.

I nod and hand the book back. Then, in typical teenage form, Olivia shifts her attention from her book and walks over to a display containing a crystal which looks to be tied to clear fishing line. "Look at this, Dad. It's beautiful. Can I get it, please?"

After paying for Olivia's crystal, we get back in the car and head to the cabin. Enroute, Olivia opens her new book and flips through it then stops and reads an excerpt out loud. "Since ancient times, dogs are believed to be in tune with the supernatural world and can detect spirits. Once they smell or see a spirit, they behave erratically, barking and whining in an attempt to warn their masters."

I nod, "Yes. I think I saw something like that in the book. Strange, don't you think?"

She shakes her head, "Kind of, but I think it's great too. After seeing that awful red demon ghost in my room, I don't think I can sleep in there again. But, if I had a dog, I would feel a lot safer and I wouldn't freak out so badly."

I laugh, "Olivia, nice try. We have no room in our lives for an animal. Don't forget, we live in the city and we're both very busy.

You're at school and I work a full week at the office. That's not fair to any animal, let alone a dog who requires a lot of attention."

Olivia sighs, "But that wouldn't be a problem. My friend Lissie at school has a Portuguese Water dog that her family puts in doggy daycare during the day and they pick up the dog on their way home. Lissie said that her dog can't wait to go to daycare because of all the other dogs to play with there."

I shake my head, "I just don't think it's the right time. Getting a dog is a huge commitment and considering what we've been through over the past 2 months..."

"That's just it, Dad. We've both been through so much. And I know I've caused you to worry a lot, and I am sorry for that. But if I could have a dog, I promise you that I would try really hard not to do stupid things or cause you anymore stress," she pauses and gives me a pleading look. "We've lost Mom and that's left an emptiness in both of us. I really need this Dad. And I promise that if we get a dog while we're on the Island, not only will I feel safer going to sleep at night, but I know it would help me to heal my heart."

I briefly take my eyes off the road and focus on her pleading face. She looks desperate and honest, and I can tell this isn't her typical *get her own way* rant when she wants something.

"At least tell me that you'll consider it. Please?" Her voice cracks with emotion.

I unbend enough to smile at her. "I'll consider it."

Olivia waits until we're parked in the cabin driveway before she wraps her arms around my chest. "Thank you, Dad. You don't know what this means to me.

Once we're inside, Olivia takes my new book and sits on the couch to read while I take my laptop and phone into my room to touch base with the office.

After about 30 minutes, I'm just finishing up on the phone with one off my firms junior lawyers when Olivia raps on my door. "Dad. I need to talk to you. It's super urgent."

She sounds panicked and out of breath. What now? Did she see that terrible red orb again? I push my laptop aside and sprint across the floor. Once I open the door, my fears instantly diminish, Olivia is bouncing up and down in front of me with anticipation, reminding me of her at 3 years old when after she would wait too long to go to the bathroom and she would do an excited pee dance. I exhale with relief. "What's going on?"

"Dad. I'm serious. You've got to come see what I found, I'm not even kidding!"

I follow the whirling dervish down the hallway into the living room. She retrieves her cell phone from the couch and shows me the screen displaying a brown and white curly-haired dog.

"Isn't he cute, Dad?"

"What breed?"

"Lagotto Romagnolo. They're originally from Italy. They're called truffle dogs, but originally they were bird retrievers. And they're super smart dad, and they don't shed."

"Why are you showing me this one now?"

"Because I thought you should know that there's a male available, he's beautiful and he's perfect and we're going to see him at 6 o'clock tonight in Parksville."

Taken aback, I look at my 14-year-old jumping bean. "I hope you're joking. You didn't really make an appointment to view a dog with out asking me first, did you?"

Olivia's shoulders slump as all of the energy drains out of her, "I guess I thought you'd be okay with just seeing the dog. Besides, it's not like we have anything else to do today."

"That's not the point, and you know it."

She frowns, "Fine. I'll just call the breeder back and cancel." She turns her back to me and punches a number on her phone then places her cell to her ear.

As much as I'm not impressed with the way she went about this, it would be nice to drive to Parksville and have a look around the beachside village.

"Okay. Alright. We can go. But don't expect to be bringing a dog home with us. Get that idea out of your head right now."

She turns to me and smiles and then wraps her arms tightly around my waist. "Thanks, Dad. And you're right, I won't expect anything. Unless of course you fall madly in love with him and want to keep him," she giggles.

* * *

In the car and driving out of Comox, Olivia punches in the directions to West Coast Lagotto in Parksville. "I spoke to the

137

lady on the phone. She's the breeder, and she's super nice. You're gonna love her dad. Her name is Debbie. You won't even believe how nice she is. She asked me a lot of questions about where we live and if we have enough space and time for a dog. I could totally tell that she cares for her animals," Olivia says, without taking a breath.

I can't help but laugh. It's been far too long since I saw her behave like a little kid. As we drive down the Island Highway, she gives me the complete breakdown of the Lagotto breed. And I must admit that even though I'm being careful not to react to what she's telling me since I don't want to get her hopes up, the Lagotto breed does have an interesting backstory.

Olivia doesn't stop chattering until we enter the small farm property. Once we pull up to a gate, she jumps out of the car and calls the breeder, Debbie, on her phone. A few moments later the gate opens, and Olivia jumps back into the car. We follow the drive to a very lovely old farm house, with a large and welcoming front porch. As soon as we get out of the car the front door opens and a woman followed by four Lagotto dogs and three little puppies steps out onto the porch. Olivia squeals with excitement and sprints toward the animals as the woman approaches me and holds out her hand. "Hi, I'm Debbie," She introduces herself. "Nice to meet you Debbie. As you can see my daughter is smitten." We both turn to watch Olivia roll around and giggle with the dogs. Debbie points to one of the Lagotto's, a beautiful male who looks like he just walked off of the cover of Show Dogs weekly, a beautiful brown and white curly coat and an aesthetic body shape.

"What's his name?" I ask.

"Winston." She smiles. "He's four. His owner got ill and reluctantly had to surrender him back to me as she couldn't physically care for him anymore."

Debbie tell me a bit more about the dog and how well trained and friendly he is, and then she calls him over to where we're standing. Olivia gets up off the ground and follows Winston as the remaining dogs follow behind.

"Hi, Debbie. Is that the one you're selling? She asks, pointing at Winston who is now leaning against me and looking up at my face. I reach down and pet his soft curly fur. Olivia walks up and leans down then wraps her arms around him. "See, Dad. Isn't he the most beautiful dog you've ever seen?"

I smile at Debbie who invites us to come into the house to discuss the adoption process.

* * *

Two hours and two cups of coffee later, Olivia, me and Winston are getting into the car. As soon as the dog is in the backseat and our seatbelts are on, Debbie waves and then opens the gate and we drive out. Olivia puts her hand on mine, "I am so happy Dad. I love you so much. I will take great care of Winston. I'll walk him tons and clean up after him, and I'll be the best dog mom in the whole world." Her face is animated and full of excitement. I wish Laura was alive to see our daughter so happy.

By the time we get back to the cabin, Winston is laying down and sleeping on the backseat, somehow he went from looking like a medium-sized dog to a sprawling beast who takes up most of the backseat. Olivia gets out of the car and immediately lets the dog out then leads him to a spot of grass to pee while I open the door to the cabin and walk inside.

Chapter Ten

After a full day of Olivia and Winston bonding and running on the beach and turning the cabin upside down. I order in Chinese food and the three of us sit on the couch to wait. With Winston and Olivia all played out, the room is quiet until simultaneously, there's a rap at the door and at the same time Olivia's cell phone rings. After I meet the delivery driver and pay for our food, I walk to the kitchen to get plates and overhear the phone conversation Olivia is having.

"Oh, that's wonderful, Grandma. I'd love to." She covers the receiver and tells me that her grandmother has found pictures of her mother and has asked if Olivia can spend the night. "I really want to get some pictures of mom." Olivia says pleading. "Can I go?"

I shrug and then motion toward Winston. "Are you sure you want to leave him so soon?"

She shakes her head and then presses a finger over her mouth to shush me. Once she ends the call, she tells me that when her grandma comes to pick her up, she'll introduce Winston to her and when she sees how cute he is, she'll let him go along.

As I dish out our food, I tell Olivia not to get her hopes up, "Your grandmother isn't a warm person. Don't be surprised if she won't take the dog, no matter how cute he is.

"She's going to fall in love with you," Olivia tells Winston as she kisses him on the muzzle.

We eat our dinner while Winston has a staring contest with us, trying to appeal to our kindness and get us to share our food, something neither one of us do. Once we've eaten, Olivia carries our dishes to the sink and tells me she's going to her room to pack her toothbrush and pajamas. As she walks down the hall, Winston follows close behind and it's obvious he's already bonding with her.

I make my way to the window, looking out at the moonlit sea. The water is calm, almost eerily flat, and what appears to be millions of tiny lights twinkle across the dark expanse. Mary suddenly comes to mind, and I wonder how she's doing—and whether she ever found her heirloom necklace. Once Greta picks up Olivia, I plan to head down to the beach, where I'm hoping to run into my mysterious new friend.

Fifteen minutes later, Olivia and Winston emerge from the bedroom and head toward the front door. Olivia stops and wraps her arms around me, planting a kiss on my cheek. "Winston is the best thing that's happened to me since we lost mom," she says "thank you for getting him for me."

A horn beeps outside and Olivia reaches down and clips the leash on Winston's collar and then slings her bag over her shoulder,

"Grandma's here. See ya in the morning, Dad." She smiles then heads out to the waiting car.

I walk over and look out of the small window in the door. Greta is perched behind the wheel of her compact car and is saying something to Olivia who is standing with Winston with the passenger door open. A moment later, Olivia walks back toward the house with the dog behind her. I quickly returned to the couch as I didn't want her to know that I'd been spying.

The door opens and Olivia sighs, "Dad. She won't let Winston go to her house. She told me to bring him inside and then called him a stinking beast." Her eyes well up. "I swear dad, if I didn't want to get the pictures of mom as badly as I do, I would tell her that if she doesn't want Winston around then I don't want to be around her!"

I nod. "You have to do what's right for you, kid. As for Greta, she's not the most welcoming person, to say the least. I'm not at all surprised that she doesn't like dogs. If its any conciliation, she doesn't like people too much either."

A tear falls down her cheek. "I wish I could stay here with you and Winston. But I can't. I'll stay the night and then get up early and come home. Then, the next time she asks me to go to her place, I'll say no."

I feel sad for her. But in this situation, it's her choice. Miserable old Greta should've had the pictures of Laura copied and then dropped them off for Olivia, instead of using the photos as a lure to get Olivia to spend time with her, but there's not much I can do. If someone was holding pictures of my mother, there's nothing I wouldn't do to get them. Olivia hugs Winston then unhooks his leash, "See you tomorrow, boy." She says, sniffing back tears.

Feeling compelled to lighten her mood, I say, "Tell Greta that next time she comes over that she should just ride her broom. It'll be cheaper than driving her car."

Olivia laughs, "I wish I had the guts."

* * *

Once Olivia is gone, Winston and I get into an intense staring contest. When I was a child, we had Max, a retriever who would communicate by using the same stare as Winston is giving me now. Usually, Max's glare meant he was bored and wanted to be either fed or to go for a walk. Since Winston has already woofed back a healthy portion of kibble, it's a safe bet he wants me to take him outside. As I put on my shoes, I get the feeling that although Olivia is madly in love with this creature, I'll be the one walking him most of the time.

Thankfully, the weather is agreeable and there's no wind blowing as we make our way along the path toward the beach. As soon as Winstons paws hit the sand, he lunges toward the water. It takes a surprising amount of power to hold him back. I'm shocked that Olivia could hold onto him during their walks today. "Slow down, boy." I say, as my feet drag in the sand.

Once we reach the water, Winston digs in the compact sand near the waters edge, I move out of the way as shovels of dirt pass between his back legs as he grunts and claws. He is definitely a high-energy breed and our lives are going to need a major over-hauling to accommodate him back in Vancouver. The penthouse is definitely out. We'll need a spacious yard so he can have lots of room to run. He seems to love the beach so I guess I should call a realtor and check out what's available for beachfront properties.

Winston suddenly stops digging and pivots around staring into the darkening beach. His body seems frozen like a statue as he focuses on something in the distance. "What's the matter, boy?" I ask, stroking his rigid head.

Then, from out of the shadows, a willowy figure emerges and walks toward us.

Winston starts to whine, and as the figure draws nearer, his volume increases and his whining changes to barking and yelping. Once I realize that the approaching person is Mary I do my best to calm the dog, but to no avail, as Mary's approach seems to drive Winston into a frenzy.

"We got a dog. He's really very sweet. I have no idea why he's acting this way." I yell.

Mary slows to a stop while I hold Winston back.

"I'll take him back to the cabin," I tell her, "just give me a few moments and I'll be right back. I've been wanting to talk to you. Using all of my strength, I maneuver Winston across the beach, and once we're alongside the cabin, he settles and the tension on the leash relaxes. Inside, I give him a bowl of water, take his collar off and head back out to meet with Mary. When I reach her , I apologize for the dog's strange behavior. She smiles and sluffs off the incident, telling me that a lot of animals act that way around her. I find it strange as she has a very friendly demeanor and there's nothing physical about her willowy frame that poses a threat, but I shrug and turn my attention to Mary, who asks me why I haven't been around for the past couple of nights and then mentions Olivia.

"You agreed to bring her to me so I could speak with her. I don't think you understand how bad things could get."

"It's really not like that anymore. Olivia has completely turned around. And I'm positive all of that weird witchcraft stuff has gone by the wayside. She's a normal…"

Mary's eyes furrow, "No. It's not that easy. Your daughter may have changed but the danger hasn't. She conjured up something evil with her friends and trust me, no matter how much her behaviour has changed makes no difference. The beings they conjured up are here now, and they have no intention to leave until they get what they came for."

I'm dumbfounded and a little weirded out by what she's saying. I take a second and try to think of a response. "Umm. I'm not quite sure I follow you. What exactly are you saying? And who was conjured up? I'm sorry but I have to admit, I'm a little concerned for you."

She shakes her head and sighs, "Yeah. I thought this would be your reaction. Let me try to explain this another way. Both you and Olivia saw the spirits, correct?"

"Well, I'm not exactly sure what we saw."

"You're a smart man, Oliver. You run a law firm in the city and no doubt have gained a lot of respect among your peers. Your brains have earned you success, so, why is it that you can't figure out what you saw in the cabin?"

I take a deep breath. "I'm not sure. Maybe there's a good explanation, one I have yet to consider."

"I don't think that's true. If you thought the strange glowing energies you saw were easily explained, then why did you visit a church for answers?"

My mouth involuntarily drops open. "How did you know about that? Were you following me?" I say, feeling defensive.

Mary reaches out and touches my arm, "I'm sorry. I'm not trying to upset you its just that we don't have a lot of time before something else happens, something that could harm you and your daughter. I wouldn't want that to happen to either of you."

My first instinct is to tell her that she's out of her mind and suggest that she get some professional help, but instead I take a moment and respond calmly, "Mary. You seem like a very nice person, I've enjoyed walking with you on the beach at night, but I think you may be worried about something that isn't real. I mean no disrespect to you and I appreciate that you are concerned for my daughter and me, but there's really no need. We're fine."

She stares deeply into my eyes. "We're wasting time," she says "time that we don't have. If you don't let me speak to Olivia so I can find out exactly what she did when she and her friends held that seance, I may not be able to protect you."

It's clear Mary isn't about to let this go. In fact, she seems to be getting more insistent, her eyes wide with urgency as she talks about these "dangerous spirits" that supposedly have it out for Olivia and me. I'm not buying any of it, and there's no way in hell I'll introduce her to Olivia, especially with how wild her theories are getting. I don't want my daughter having any weird thoughts planted in her head now that she's finally started acting normal again. I politely tell Mary that I should get back to the cabin as we haven't had the dog very long and I'm not sure how he'll deal with being left alone.

Mary looks upset and turns to face the water. "Don't say I didn't warn you." She mumbles.

"Goodnight, Mary," I say, as I turn and head back to the cabin.

* * *

Sitting on the couch with Winston curled up against me, my eyes catch the book I borrowed from the library, The Dark Past of The Comox Valley, the same book I was reading when Olivia interrupted me once she had finished shopping. I thumb through the pages until I get to where I left off, a story about an exceptionally beautiful young indigenous woman who was well liked in the community. As I read, I learned about how during the mid eighteen hundreds during the time of the first settlers, a European man met the woman known as Dancing Mary and the two were married.

It wasn't long before the man, who was known to have a quick temper, grew jealous of how many men's heads his young wife turned within in the settlement. One night,

154

while the moon was full, the angry settler lost his temper with his wife, and it wasn't long after that night that people started to realize the young woman had gone missing. Most of the settlers believed that she had fallen victim to her husband's rage. For weeks, the women and men of the village searched for her but to no avail, her body was never recovered. Even though there was little doubt that the jealous husband had killed his wife, no body was ever found and he was never brought to justice. Years passed and although there were always whispers about what may have become of Mary, nothing was ever done to solve the mystery. That is, until a young soldier who was riding his bicycle along dark and desolate Comox Ave, said he saw a glowing blue light. Unable to stop on such short notice, the soldier rode the bike straight through the blue light. Later, he gave a statement about the incident where he mentioned that passing through the blue light gave him a freezing cold sensation, one he had never felt before.

I look up from my book and notice that Winston has suddenly risen from his place on the rug, and turned around in a tight circle before lying back down. As I resume reading, I think about Mary, not the woman from the story, but Mary, my new friend from the beach and how unfortunate it is that she had to turn out to be somewhat strange. I guess I should've noticed signs from when I first met her on the beach, how this beautiful young indigenous woman who I only saw on the beach late at night, was walking up and down the shoreline looking for a lost necklace. It should have occurred to me that something wasn't right, why the heck would someone wait until dark to look for something as small as a piece of jewelry ? I sigh deeply. It figures the one person I am drawn to turns out to be strange.

I yawn and Winston does the same. I reach out and stroke his head. "What do you think, boy? Is it bedtime?"

I put my book down and get up to take the dog for one last pee before we retire for the night. As I stand on the steps, I look upward at the dark clouds rolling inward. Suddenly a blast of icy air rushes against me, and I tell Winston to quit sniffing around and do his business.

Once in bed, the dog takes his place beside me, and it feels like forever since I've shared my bed, and even though he's a dog, it's a comfort having him next to me. After a few slow pats, Winston lets out a huge sigh and stretches out.

* * *

A piercing yelp jerks me out of my deep sleep and I spring to a sitting position. Blinking a few times to focus, I see Winston at the bottom of the bed, barking and screeching at the closed bedroom door.

"What's the matter, boy?" I say, stroking him, and am surprised at the rigidity of his body. "Don't be scared," I say, assuming that he's heard a branch scrape on one of the cabin windows.

After unsuccessfully trying to calm him down, I decide to take him into the front room so he can see there is no threat.

"Come on, pup." I say, motioning for him to follow.

I freeze in the doorway, my heart hammering in my chest. Winston's frantic barking now sounds almost distant, drowned out by the strange, suffocating energy in the air. His growls have shifted to something softer, almost like a warning—soft whimpers, like he's unsure of what's going on. My breath catches in my throat, and the hairs on the back of my neck stand up as a cold, heavy presence washes over me, intensifying with every second.

That red glow on the ceiling—it's back. It's just like before, pulsating with an eerie light, floating above the door to Olivia's room like some kind of silent sentinel. It feels like the walls are closing in, the darkness creeping into every corner, yet there's this magnetic pull that keeps me rooted to the spot. I can't move, not yet. Not while I still don't understand what is in front of me.

What the hell is this thing, I mutter under my breath, my voice barely more than a whisper, like I'm afraid the air itself will swallow it whole.

I take a step forward, and the shape hanging in the air—gets darker, shifting and impossible to fully grasp, it makes my pulse race faster, and my skin crawls as though it's alive.

I want to turn and run back into my room, lock the door, and pretend this isn't happening. But something holds me in place. It's not just fear. It's a feeling deep in my gut, a need to understand, to confront whatever this is before Olivia comes back.

She won't be able to handle another scary encounter. Not if it's the same thing that terrified her before.

I take another shaky step, my eyes locked on the glowing light. Whatever this thing is, it's not just a figment of my imagination—it's real, and there's a suffocating, malevolent force radiating from it. My gut twists with a mix of fear and determination. I need answers. I need to figure out what the hell this is.

"Why are you here? What do you want?" My voice is trembling as I pull my shoulders back to fane bravery.

My eyes fixate on the crimson mass, waiting for it to move or better yet, leave. Winston is crouched about a foot from my feet, I briefly look at him and think how much like a statue he looks. He's afraid to move, unsure what to do next, much like me.

Then, without warning, the thing starts to pulsate and expand, I catch myself stepping backward while looking down so as not to step on the dog. When I look back up at the ceiling, the mass has disappeared. I draw in a deep breath, the first one I've had since the strange thing appeared. I turn to walk into the bedroom to get my housecoat when I feel an eerie and powerful energy behind me, almost like electricity surging through me and up the back of my neck. I'm instantly reminded of when I was young and my friends and me would hide in the dark and try and scare each other. No matter how quiet they were, I always felt it when one of them was behind me, it's the same feeling I have right now.

I know I have to turn and look but I'm terrified, it takes every bit of mental strength to will my body to move. Winston whines and then jumps on the bed and darts toward the headboard and settles on the pillows.

Slowly, I turn with my whole body in tremors.

I let out a gasp when my eyes focus on the strange figure of what looks like a blurry image of a man. He appears taller than I am, and he seems spirit-like with his feet floating a few inches above the floor. I try to yell but no noise comes out of my mouth. I stare in disbelief, as the figure becomes more defined and distinctive. His face is long and drawn and ashen. He has a dark beard, and his eyes are as black as coal. Suddenly, he steps toward me, and my heart pounds in my chest. I'm trying to speak when the mans mouth opens and his lips move side to side like he's chewing something. Then, his lips thin and his mouth spreads into an evil sneer as it opens wide to reveal burning red ember lodged in the back of his throat. I gasp in horror as his mouth becomes a cavern, and I stare at the blazing cinder inside the dark cave of his throat. I try to move my feet but they won't budge, I'm frozen where I stand. Suddenly, the evil being darts towards me and his blood curdling shriek rents the air, "From hell I have escaped to drag her bones to the grave."

As suddenly as it appeared the image turns to vapor and disappears. I suck in air through my constricted lungs and cough repeatedly. Unable to think clearly or to form words, I let out a grunt. My mind is spinning, but I don't doubt what I saw, there's no question that no matter how surreal or unexplainable it was, A ghost, or an evil spirit has come with a driven purpose, and he intends to take someone with him to whichever realm he came from. Slowly, I make my way to the living room, periodically using the wall to support my trembling legs. Olivia, I need to get myself together and then gather all of our things and pack them in the car so when Olivia comes home, we can leave this place and head back to the city, far away from this nightmare.

Chapter Eleven

Dawn crawls over the horizon and casts a golden glow through the cabin windows. With the sign of daybreak, Winston is more willing to go outside and pee. Thankfully, his body has relaxed and he has stopped shivering. I feel guilty for taking him away from his peaceful home with the breeder and bringing him here, exposing him to the evil occurrence that happened last night.

After a quick pee and a few sniffs around the narrow lawn, the dog comes back inside and follows me as I pull bags and suitcases from the closets and open them on the beds to start packing. I start with Olivia's room and shovel armloads of her clothes from the dresser to her duffel bag. After emptying two drawers, I open the last one and am in the midst of grabbing more clothes when my hand hits something long and hard on the bottom of the drawer.

I move the garments out of the way and look down at a red wooden box with the words Ouija etched on the front in gothic black lettering. What in the hell is this? Was Olivia messing around with a Ouija board as well as witchcraft? And if so, why does she still have it in her drawer, especially after she confessed everything to me. I thought she was done with all of this crazy spirit stuff. I exhale loudly, once we get back to the city, I'm making her another appointment with a therapist. This time, she won't be clamming up and refusing to talk either. Enough is enough.

Leaving the game board in the drawer, I finish emptying the dresser and packing her suitcase. With Winston watching, I gather all of our belongings and start packing the car. A few minutes later, Greta pulls up with Olivia. Once the car comes to a complete stop, Olivia spots Winston and jumps out of the car and runs over to greet Winston who is just as excited to see her. Greta yells at Olivia to shut the passenger door. Once the door is closed, Greta backs out of the driveway without waving or acknowledging my presence. Typical.

"Dad, what are you doing?" Olivia finally notices the bags in the open trunk.

"I'm packing our stuff. So, you should go inside and make sure I got everything of yours from your room."

Olivia shakes her head and puts her hands on her hips, "I'm not going anywhere. Grandma is going to let me go through my moms stuff in the attic tomorrow."

I take a deep breath and try to be diplomatic. "She will have to send you the stuff. It's time that we go home."

Immediately, Olivia shifts her arms to her chest and crosses them, "Fine. You can leave and Winston and me will stay here. And when I'm done at grandma's, I'll come back to Vancouver."

"You're being ridiculous. I'm not leaving you here and even if I did, you'll have no way back to the city, especially with a dog."

Olivia's eyes well up. "I'm taking Winston for a walk on the beach because if I stay here right now, I'm going to say something really bad." She stalks away, and knowing that there's no way I'm getting her to come peacefully with me right now, I decide not to pursue the matter until we've both calmed down. I close the trunk and walk inside as Olivia and Winston disappear around the house.

Back inside, I walk over to the window and stare out over the beach just as my daughter and the dog enter my view. Winston is sprinting ahead of Olivia and then turning and running back to her. She chases him as he playfully barks and spins around in the sand. Then, something appears to catch the duo's attention and they walk out of view.

As much as I don't want to separate Olivia from the possibility of getting belongings of her mother from Greta, after what happened last night, my experience with what I am now sure to be an evil spirit, I don't want to stay here another night in case it returns, especially since Olivia will be here.

I do a sweep through the cabin, meticulously looking for anything of mine that was left unpacked. Twenty minutes later, I'm washing my face when I hear Olivia come through the front door, "Dad!"

Her voice is full of excitement, but there's an edge of anxiety to it. I quickly dry my face and step into the hall just as she's coming toward me. "Dad," she says, breathing heavily. "The weirdest thing just happened. I met this strange lady on the beach. She knew my name—and even Winston's."

My first thought is Mary.

"Let's go and sit in the living room." I motion her back down the hall.

Once we're seated on the couch, I calmly ask her what the woman said to her.

Olivia's eyes widen and in typical teenage dramatic form, she goes on to tell me how the beautiful woman called her name on the beach and then started to talk to her about really confusing things.

"Like what?" I ask.

"I think she knew about the weird spirit that I saw, Dad. She kept talking about an evil entity and even mentioned that it was red, which it was. How could she know that?"

Thankfully, I don't have to try and come up with an answer because Olivia continues to ramble nervously. "Then, she asked me what I did with my friends before the spirit revealed itself to me. It was so weird, Dad! It really freaked me out." Olivia brushed a rogue hair from her face with a trembling hand. "I mean...how the heck does she know all of that stuff about me, anyway?"

I take a long breath and then lean back onto the couch. "The woman's name is Mary."

"You know her?" Olivia says with surprise.

I shrug, "I wouldn't say that I know her but we've had conversations while I was on the beach."

Olivia's expression changes from fear to annoyance as her brows furrow, "So, is that how she knew my name and Winston's? And what about the weird stuff she was asking about, the séance I had with those kids? You told her that too?"

I know how much my daughter hates it when I talk about her, she's always been very sensitive that way, but seeing no way around the truth, I tell that her name came up in idle conversation when I was on the beach with Mary.

"I can't believe you did that, Dad. How can I trust you when you tell a complete stranger personal stuff about me?"

I explain that I did not intentionally talk about her to breech her trust. "It was a fast conversation with Mary and it just kind of came up."

Olivia scoffs. "Whatever!" then she stands up and tells me that she's going to her room. Winston immediately stands and follows her.

"And I'm not leaving Comox until I get mom's stuff from my grandma." She calls out before entering her room and slamming the door.

Frustrated, I sit down on the sofa and think about what I can do to change her mind about leaving. My first instinct is to call Greta and see if she can take Olivia for another night, that way, if the evil ghost thing returns, Olivia wont see it. But, knowing Greta and her intolerance of me, if I do call her, she'll more than likely just hang up on me and I'll be no further ahead. Reluctantly, I get up and go to Olivia's room and knock softly on the door. "I have an idea.

Why don't you call your grandmother and see if you can stay there tonight and tomorrow, you and I can hash things out about when we should go back to Vancouver."

I wait for a few long moments before she answers, "Are you that sick of me?"

"Don't be silly, Olivia. I just thought since you have stuff of your mom's there, maybe you could go through some of it tonight."

"I just got home from there. Besides, grandma isn't going to be home tonight. She's going to stay with a friend until some time tomorrow."

"Alright then," I sigh with frustration and head back to living room.

* * *

A hot mist startles me out of sleep and I open my eyes to see Winston's face an inch away. I reach out and pat the top of his head and then sit up.

"Dad. I just want to tell to that I'm sorry for how I acted." Olivia says walking into view.

"It's okay." I grin, then look at the clock on the wall. It's almost dinner time and I've been sleeping for hours.

"I guess we should think about getting some dinner."

She nods.

I ask Olivia if she feels like going out to eat or if she'd rather order in, and she chooses the latter. I grab my phone and start searching for take-out options when she mentions that, while I was sleeping, she brought our bags in from the car and put them back in our rooms. It's strange how noisy teens are when they're stumbling around the house, yet when they're sneaking out or doing something they don't want you to know about, they're almost invisible.

I find an ad for The Curry Cottage nearby. After scrolling through the menu, I ask Olivia if she's interested. Given her love for spicy food, it's no surprise when she agrees. "It's a take-out place, so we'll have to go pick it up," I tell her.

Olivia shakes her head. "Considering how upset I was earlier, I'm actually feeling tired now. I think I'll stay home with Winston." She grabs my phone and scrolls through the menu, stopping at a coconut curry dish. "Tell them to make it extra spicy," she grins.

Once I've called the restaurant and placed the order, I head out to pick up our food.

* * *

I feel a bit hesitant about leaving Olivia alone at the cabin, especially with all the strange things that have been happening. But there's no talking her into coming with me. The paranormal events have all occurred in the dead of night while we were asleep, and it's only dinner time now. So, I reassure myself I won't be long—I'll grab the food and head straight back home.

As I drive up Comox Ave, I glance up at the dark clouds swirling overhead, a clear sign that a storm is brewing. In the short time we've been on the island, it's amazing how much it's rained and how dark the skies have been. Fall is typically grey in BC, especially in a rainforest, but for some reason, the weather has felt unusually turbulent since our arrival.

The Curry Cottage is clean and spacious, with a warm, welcoming vibe—something I've noticed in most of the businesses we've visited here. A friendly lady greets me when I approach the counter. After I tell her my name, and that I'm here to pick up an order, she disappears into the kitchen. I pull my phone from my pocket and text Olivia while a waiter walks past, carrying fresh, steaming dishes. The incredible aromas hit me, and my stomach rumbles with hunger.

"Are you doing okay?" I text.

"Dad. Seriously? You literally just left."

The waitress returns with my order, and I reply to Olivia with a thumbs-up emoji. On the drive back to the cabin, the wind picks up, and the car is pelted with heavy, sideways rain that makes the wipers almost useless. I slow to half the speed I was driving on the way to the restaurant, inching my way back, taking twice as long as expected.

When I finally pull into the driveway and shut off the engine, I grab the food and look through the soaked windshield. Olivia is standing on the doorstep, waving her arms frantically. My heart skips a beat, and I feel my pulse quicken, wondering what could've happened in the short time I've been gone.

I quickly lock the car door and sprint toward her. "What's wrong? What happened? Are you okay?"

"You're not going to believe this, Dad. Wait til I tell you what I found."

"Found? Where? Inside?" I ask worriedly.

"Come inside and I'll show you."

She opens the door and walks inside. After we're both in, I set the food on the counter and turn to see her on the couch with an open book on her lap. "Dad, look," she says tapping on a page, it's her."

"It's whom?"

"The lady from the beach, Mary."

I walk over and take the book from her then see the heading, Dancing Mary.

"This is the library book I signed out when we were in Courtenay. It's tales of ghosts and other things that can't be proven."

"No, Dad. Read what it says about the pretty indigenous lady who was murdered and her body was never found. Her name was Mary."

I grin and shake my head as I hand her the book and return to the kitchen to get our food. "A lot of people are named Mary. Besides, the lady from the beach is real, not a ghost and more importantly, the lady they called dancing Mary lived in the mid 1800s, not in our time."

"Dad. Don't you find it at all weird that the Mary from the beach is so preoccupied with what we both saw here in the cabin? And then how she just appeared on the beach while I was walking Winston and how she said all of that weird stuff to me?

"She is a bit strange; I'll give you that, but that doesn't make her a ghost. You've been watching too many scary movies."

"I knew you wouldn't believe me." Olivia's voice drops.

I walk over and hand her the curry dish. "It's not that I think you're telling me a lie, I just don't want you filling your head with a bunch of mumbo jumbo is all."

Olivia gets up and tells me that she wants to eat in her room then scuffles away with the dog on her heels.

As I eat my meal—probably the best curry I've had in a long time, which is saying something considering I'm from Vancouver, a city with some of the most acclaimed Indian restaurants on the five-star circuit—I make a mental note to talk to Olivia about that strange, spooky game she has in her dresser. As much as I'd rather avoid a confrontation, I know I need to tell her that there can be no more witchcraft or black magic-related things in our home, no matter where we are.

Once I finish my meal, I clean up, double-check that the door is locked, and head to my room. As I pass Olivia's door, I knock softly. When there's no response after a few moments, I whisper, "Good night," before heading to my own room.

After changing into my pajamas, I lie on the bed, staring at the ceiling, praying that whatever that strange, angry orb was, it doesn't make another appearance. At least Olivia has Winston with her, no matter how timid he is.

* * *

I'm jolted awake by a faint cry coming from somewhere in the house. I sit up, glancing at the digital clock on the nightstand—it's 2 a.m. Hoping it's just a dream, I strain to listen, waiting for the sound to return. A few moments pass, and then I hear it again, this time louder. "Help me! Daddy, help me!" The eerie softness of Olivia's voice wraps around me, sending a chill down my spine.

I spring to my feet, rushing into the hallway toward Olivia's room. I grab the door handle, but it won't budge. There's no lock on the door, just a weathered old knob, so there's no reason it should be stuck.

"Daddy, hurry. He's coming for me, and I'm scared," her faint voice comes from inside the room.

"Open the door, Olivia!" I can't get in. I yell.

"Daddy, please help me."

My mind is spinning and my body is full of anxiety and fear for my little girl. I bang on the door with both fists. "Olivia, open the door. You have to open the door! I holler.

Then, I hear another voice in the room, a haunting raspy voice that booms from inside the room. Olivia screams, "Noooo, please go away. Please stop."

With my fists and my feet, punching and kicking on the door, I yell as loudly as I can, "Don't you touch her. Stay away from her you son of a bitch! Then, an instant quiet falls over the cabin. All I can hear is my pounding heart and my lungs gasping for air. I reach out and grab the door handle and it turns with ease. Terrified of what I'm about to see, I push open the door. Immediately, I rush towards the bed where I find Olivia sleeping on her side with Winston peacefully curled up at her feet. He lifts his head as I step closer, and then with disinterest, lowers his head back down onto the blanket. I bend over my daughter and put my hand on her shoulder, listening for the sounds of her breath. Her body shifts lightly under my touch and her eyes flutter open. "Dad. Why are you in here? What's going on?" Her voice is groggy and faint.

Both confused and relieved, I tell her that everything is okay and to go back to sleep. When I take my hand off her shoulder, I notice blood on the white fabric of her nightie. I look at my knuckles and see where the skin has split and blood is oozing out. I look at my other fist and it's the same thing; I must've split my hands open when I was bashing on the door. Thankfully, Olivia doesn't notice and lowers her head back down on her pillow. I pull up the blanket to cover her and am just backing away when her eyes fly open and she sits up and screams, "Daddy. Look," her voice rises in terror and she points behind me. Winston jumps up and starts barking in the direction of the door.

I whip around and an icy shiver runs through my veins. A blast of fiery red pulsates in front of me. I shift my feet so my body is hiding my daughter. Winston keeps barking and Olivia continues to scream but their voices sound distant and far away as I stare at the thing in front of me.

"Go away!" I try to yell, but my voice comes out a trembling whisper.

A face forms in the flaming red light. The face is evil, pure evil, and when it opens its mouth it emits a blast of demonic sound, almost like a twisted laughter. "Out of my way," it roars

I shake my head and am just about to speak when from the hallway there comes a blood curdling scream and a bright blue glow fills the door way. The evil red demon snaps around in response to the scream then shoots through the doorway and into the hall. I gather my wits and grab Olivia's arm, "Let's go. Hurry."

"Where?" she sobs.

I point to the window then lead her across the bed. With the dog going crazy, barking and yelping, I reach the window, still hanging onto to my daughter's arm. Grabbling the latch, I try to turn it so I can open the window and make our escape but it wont budge.

"Dad hurry before it comes back!"

"I'm trying, honey." I say, straining to move the metal latch.

As I push and pull on the handle, flashes of red and blue flash around the room followed by bone chilling screeches that echo up and down the hallway.

"Dad. Hurry. Please!"

The latch won't budge. The terrifying reality hits me, we're going to have to get past those battling orbs and run for the front door of the cabin. I turn to Olivia and grab onto her shoulders, "Sweetie, listen to me. We're going to have to make a run for it through the hallway and out the front door."

Her eyes widen with terror, "No. I can't. I can't go out there, that evil thing will get me."

"No. I won't let anything happen to you but you've got to move fast with me, okay? Just hold onto me as tightly as you can and you'll be okay."

She starts to cry "No. No. I can't. I'm too scared. You go and I'll stay here!"

I tighten my grip on her shoulders and stare into her eyes. "You're not staying here. We're doing this together and we're going to be fine!" I don't know if it's true, but I'm desperate to convince her.

Finally, her feet start to move and she latches both hands onto my forearm. "I'm so scared, Dad. I don't want to die."

"You're not going to Die, Olivia. I won't let anything happen to you."

Panic surges through me as I put my arms around Olivia and lead her across the floor Once we reach the doorway, I tell Olivia to keep her head down and to not let go of me. Her hands are shaking as she tightens her grip on my arm.

We enter the hallway, and my eyes are drawn to the ceiling where the red and blue orbs or spirits are zipping past each other. It is obvious from their sharp thrusts and shrill shrieks, that they are locked in battle, and we need to get out of there before they turn their attention back to us. I take a deep breath and whisper to my daughter, "okay, Olivia. Remember what I told you, don't let go of me."

The aggressive energy swoops over our heads, screaming and screeching as they careen into the ceiling and the walls.

"Come, Winston." Olivia urges our dog, and then breaks out in sobs, "They're going to get us, Dad. I know they are."

"Don't think like that, just be quiet and keep walking."

I can hear Olivia sniffling as we near the door. Winston seems to sense we're headed for the exit—he stops barking and trots ahead of us. We're only about ten feet from the front door now. I grip the door handle, silently praying that what happened before, when I tried to get into Olivia's room and the handle wouldn't turn, doesn't happen again. One foot closer, then another. So far, so good. Please, let us make it.

Suddenly, Winston stops dead in his tracks, his ears perked, eyes wide, as he looks behind us down the hallway. He starts shrill barking, just as I hear it—a bone-chilling, guttural yell growing louder and closer. I want to look, to see what's coming, but I can't. I'm too terrified.

"Dad!" Olivia yells. "It's coming!"

"It's okay, Olivia, just stay close and don't look."

The sinister roaring soon grows unbearably loud, drowning out the dog's barking. I glance at the door, only a few steps away, and take one more step forward. Suddenly, it hits—a shockwave of force so powerful it knocks Olivia's hand from my arm, separating us.

I look over at my daughter, who has been thrown to the floor, and see the evil red demon hovering over her. As terrified as I am, I can't let it take her. I'm about to lunge toward her when I notice the powerful blue glow of the spirit rushing along the wall toward us.

As the red demon moves closer to Olivia, the blue orb strikes it hard from the side. I spring forward, landing with my arms around Olivia just as the two spirits clash, twisting and bouncing off the walls. They separate for only a moment before the blue orb charges at the red one again, this time seeming to weaken the crimson demon. With a flash, the red spirit vanishes into the walls.

I help Olivia to her feet, and the blue orb floats slowly toward us, coming to a stop just above our heads. I stare into it as it hovers silently. Then, Winston barks, startling the pulsating blue energy. It zooms down the hall and dissolves into the ceiling.

I take a deep breath, holding Olivia tightly. We start to move toward the door when a loud knock echoes through the cabin.

Winston runs to the door and barks as we approach. I reach out and grab onto the handle, thankfully, the knob turns and the door opens.

Chapter Twelve

I jump back, gasping as I see the figure standing on the doorstep. With Winston barking furiously and Olivia trying to push past me, it takes a moment before I recognize the stranger—it's Mary.

"What are you doing here?" I snap, trying to get a hold of Winston.

There's a severity in her eyes and she takes a step toward me, "You're both in grave danger. I need to speak with you now."

"What you need to do is to get out of the way. My daughter and I are leaving."

Mary shakes her head. "You don't understand. You can't just leave and expect the evil spirit not to follow you, it wants your daughter, not this cabin."

"What in the hell are you going on about. What we need to do is get out of here."

"If you go away, I cannot protect you, I am bound to these shores until my people come and free me."

"Mary, you sound crazy."

She frowns and then grabs my free arm, "And what just happened to you both, what you saw doesn't strike you as crazy? I realize that I am not the image of a big strong person, but I am the only thing that stands between the bad spirit and your daughter. And believe me, he will do everything he can to take her."

"Take her?" I scoff. "What do you mean by that?"

Mary leans in closer, "You saw the way he hovered over her, how he locked her bedroom door so you couldn't get inside.

How in the hell did she know what happened?

"He is crafty and evil and his power grows with every day he is free. You must listen to what I am telling you. I need to come inside. I need to speak with Olivia."

I'm just about to tell Mary to move out of our way when to my surprise, Olivia says, "Dad. I think we have to trust her. She knows about the spirit world. Remember what it said in the book? It's her dad, I know it. She's Dancing Mary."

"Please. Let me in and I can explain things."

"I don't want my daughter or me to be in this cabin as long as that evil thing is nearby."

"It's gone now. You are safe here for the time being, trust me."

Olivia taps on my shoulder and sobs, "Please, Dad. She's the only hope we have of making that demon thing stay away from us."

Her words sound absurd and unbelievable, but then again, so does what we saw here tonight. Besides, Mary's statement that the evil orb will follow us is terrifying. I motion for her to come inside. "I guess at this point we haven't much to lose. What's your plan, Mary?"

"Olivia has a board that was used to conjure up her mother. Someone else, a powerful spirit came through instead. I need to see the board, and I need her to tell me exactly what happened while she was using it."

"Do you mean that a random evil spirit came through?"

"I'm hoping that's the case."

"What are you saying? What if the spirit isn't random? Are you thinking it's a soul of someone you know?"

Mary shakes her head, "I pray that's not the case. For now, I need to look at that board before I come to a conclusion."

Olivia sighs audibly, "If what I did while using that board caused that scary beast to show up, I'm not sure I want to use it again. What if more bad things start to happen?"

Mary looks at her and calmly tells her that because of what's happening, she has no choice."

Even though alarm bells are going off in my head, I step aside and let Mary follow Olivia to her room.

* * *

After about twenty minutes of pacing the living room while Mary and Olivia are behind the closed door of Olivia's room, I hear the knob on the door open and out walks Mary with a troubled expression. Olivia follows close behind as the two walk down the hall and into the front room looking scared and confused.

"What happened?"

"It was so scary, Dad. Mary asked me to set up the board the way I did when I was with my friends. Then, I told her how we all put our hands on the glass piece and then asked the board questions. But when Mary touched one side of the glass piece and I touched the other, she asked who came through the spirit world the last time the board was used and then...and then..." her voice is trembling so much she has to take a moment to compose herself. "And then the piece started to move by itself, even after we took our hands away."

Mary's eyes are staring off into the distance as though she's deep in thought.

"And then what happened?"

"The glass moved across the board and stopped on different letters."

"Which letters? What did it spell?"

She shakes her head, "I don't know, Dad. I was too freaked out."

"Thomas Cotton." Mary whispers

"Who's Thomas Cotton? This doesn't make any sense."

Mary turns to me and makes eye contact. "An evil man who lived many years ago."

"But how do you know this?"

Mary turns and walks toward the door. "He's gaining more power with every day he is freed. He must be sent back before it's too late."

"What the hell do you mean by too late?"

Mary grabs the door handle and then turns to us, "If he's not stopped soon, he will become too powerful to stop and your daughter will be in grave danger."

Olivia bursts out in tears as Mary opens the door. "You can't leave us. What if it comes back?"

In a monotone voice with her back to us she tells us that his spirit isn't near and she needs to use this time to think about what to do next.

"I'd advise you to stay together and if possible, stay in the same room with Olivia." Mary says before stepping off of the porch and disappearing into the night.

I walk across the floor and close the door and then tell Olivia to sit on the sofa with me to have a talk.

Winston jumps up on the couch followed by Olivia who slumps down looking defeated. When I sit down, I reach out and touch her shoulder. "I can't tell you what is going on here, or what it all means, but I can promise you that I won't let any harm come to you. I promise you that."

She looks over at me, her eyes filling with tears, "I'm so scared, Dad. And I feel so bad because I now know for sure that I caused all of this. It's my fault. Just ask Mary."

I shake my head and tell her that none of this is because of her doing. And as far as Mary goes, I'm not sure what to believe or not believe about what she says. "There's a very distinct possibility that she's just a woman who's lost her mind."

Olivia shakes her head, "No dad. You weren't in my room. You didn't see what I saw. That glass piece really did move by itself. And even though I don't want to believe all of this stuff is really happening, it is and I don't think Mary is crazy. I think she must have some powers that connect her to the spirit world. I just wish I knew who this Thomas Cotton is, or was, and why he wants to get me."

I want to offer her some comforting words but honestly, I have no explanations and the worse part, no solutions.

Then, Olivia suddenly straightens up and looks alert, "Dad. I have an idea. Can we go to the library tomorrow morning?"

I look at her curiously. "Of course, but what for?"

"What if we did a search on Thomas Cotton? I'd feel a lot better if we could find out some information on this guy. Even though we don't have much to go on, we have his name and Mary said that he lived a long, long time ago, so if there is anything on him, the library will have a history section."

I nod in agreement, unsure what identifying this person, or ex person will do to help us but even if we don't find out anything, we'll be no farther behind.

* * *

With Olivia cocooned in her blanket sleeping next to me and Winston sprawled out between us on the bed, I only managed to get a few hours sleep. Thankfully, there were no more incidents of ghosts or crazy things happening. Olivia was right, dogs really must have a tapped in sense to another realm. The other night, Winston freaked out when the spirits were present. I think that's why I was somewhat at ease about being safe last night, he didn't act strange or even lift his head.

"Dad. Can we get breakfast while we're out? I don't feel like eating here this morning."

I agree and then remind her to take the dog out for a pee before we leave.

I'm just changing out of my pajamas and into my streetwear when I hear Olivia and Winston leave. A few moments later, I hear the front door open again.

"Dad. You've got to see this. It's super weird."

What now? Is the thought that runs through my head as I finish putting on my socks then walk into the hallway.

Olivia and Winston are standing at the entrance with the door open and a bright stream of light flooding into the kitchen. "What is it?"

"Seriously, you've got to see this." She says, motioning outside.

I slip on my shoes and follow her onto the step. There in front of us is a curved line made of a red powder spanning the front of the cabin. "What the hell is that?" I think, out loud.

"Weird, huh?" Olivia says. And it goes all around the house."

I stand staring in bewilderment for a few minutes before snapping out of it and reminding myself not to show trepidation or concern in front of my daughter. "Okay, well. Let's not worry about it. Just take Winston for a pee and we'll go."

As soon as I'm back in the cabin and alone with my thoughts, something occurs to me, what if Mary is playing tricks on us? I have no idea why she would or for what purpose, maybe she's lonely and need attention. I don't know. But what I do know is that I can't let things get any stranger. Soon, I will have to put a stop to the weirdness we have been thrust into. Once Olivia is back, she gives Winston a long hug and then we head out.

* * *

After another breakfast at what's becoming our favorite eatery, Tidal Café', 2 orders of eggs Benny, this time foregoing the hot sauce challenge, Olivia and I arrive at the Comox Library. Olivia sets her sights on the librarian, a twenty-something lady with Natalie etched on a tag that's pinned to her sweater. Straight away, Olivia starts with requests, "Do you have anything about Comox history that involves a man named, Thomas Cotton? It would be from a long, long time ago," Olivia says excitedly.

Natalie smiles and then walks over to a small bank of computers, asks Olivia to repeat the name of the person we are interested in learning about then types away on the keyboard. It doesn't take long before Natalie finds information then writes down a book title and number on a small scrap of paper and directs us to one of the tall bookcases at the back of the room. Olivia whispers to me as we walk. "Did you see the title of the book on the paper, Dad?"

I shake my head.

"The book is called Crimes on Vancouver Island's Indigenous Peoples."

"They've been taken advantage of for hundreds of years. It's awful." I whisper back.

After locating a long shelving unit at the back of the library, Olivia runs her finger along the spines of the bottom two rows. Coming up empty, she asks me to check the top shelf. Halfway through the row, I find the book—a single copy of what looks like an old publication.

Olivia's face lights up and we find a nearby table to sit at. She takes the book, flips it open, and scans the table of contents. After a moment, she sighs. "Darn it. Thomas Cotton's name isn't here, which means it's probably in one of the chapters. Now we'll have to read the whole book to find it."

A moment later, Natalie walks by and asks if we found what we were looking for. Olivia shrugs and explains that we'll need to sign the book out, as the name is likely buried somewhere inside.

Natalie smiles and asks if we have anything else to go on, an incident or time frame involving Thomas Cotton that she could look up. Olivia and I look blankly at one another.

I thank Natalie for her offer and then admit that unfortunately, we don't have any other information. Olivia elbows me, "What about the first settlers in Comox? Remember what the book from the other library we rented said? Mary was murdered by one of the first settlers."

Natalies eyes widen, "A murder? Interesting!"

I shrug. "We're history buffs, and my daughter always seems to hone in on the wildest tales."

Natalie tells us to wait while she sees if she can find any other information out on the computer.

"Do you think Winston is okay at the cottage by himself?" Olivia asks, looking concerned.

"He's fine." I assure her.

"I guess you're right." She nods. "We should see if they have a little shop around here with metaphysical stuff, like at that place we bought my crystal from. Maybe they'll have something that can fend off bad energy. Maybe we can put something on Winston's collar to protect him."

"Please lower your voice. If someone overhears you they're likely to think we're nuts."

"I think I found something," Natalie smiles as she makes her way toward us. "Follow me and I'll show you how to access it online so you don't have to spend ages thumbing through that big book."

We get up from the table and Natalie takes the book from Olivia then returns it to the shelf before leading us back to the bank of computers.

We watch as Natalie scrolls through online pages before stopping on a heading that reads, The First Settlers in The Land of Plenty.

Olivia scrunches up her face. "That doesn't sound like what we're looking for."

I nudge her to be quiet as Natalie scrolls down a few lines. Skipping every few sentences, the book goes on to mention how for thousands of years, the K'ómoks people lived in the "Land of Plenty" on Eastern Vancouver Island and how they inhabited areas like Salmon River, Quinsam River, and Comox Harbour and that their relationship with the land was rich and sustainable, relying on salmon, shellfish, herring, deer, elk, seal, and plants. Also mentioned is how the K'ómoks people would consider seashells treasures and they would gather and bury them.

"Dad, look. Look!" Olivia taps the screen. The words Murder and on the Land of Plenty jump off the page. My eyes quickly scan the text and read how a lot of early European settlers who arrived in Comox in the mid-1800s were savages, behaving like animals during wild parties and how they destroyed the land for its trees and resources, disrespecting the rightful owners—the K'ómoks people. I sigh in disgust and continue reading.

"Look, Dad." Olivia raises her voice, pointing at the last few lines. "Thomas Cotton."

"Shh."

Apparently from a small Yorkshire village in England, Cotton is listed among the first settlers who came to Comox in the mid-19th century. As we read on, we learn that he married a local K'ómoks woman not long after he arrived. The only description of the woman is that she was beautiful and kind. Her Indigenous name isn't given but the villagers called her Mary.

"Mary! Do you see that, Dad? Her name was Mary! Dancing Mary, I bet!"

Ignoring Olivia, I keep reading.

Thomas Cotton was about 30 when he first arrived in Comox and died just a year later, apparently from a mysterious illness. As far as his pretty young wife, her fate was sealed not long after she married Cotton. Though the villagers believed that Mary's life was taken by her new husband, known to have a violent nature and a jealous tendency toward his wife. Sadly, Mary's body was never recovered and Cotton was never charged with her murder.

"How did Mary die? Does it say?" Olivia asks excitedly.

I shake my head.

"See? That's why Mary mentioned Thomas Cotton! He was her ex-husband and he murdered her. That's who the evil spirit is who has been terrorizing us." Olivia says.

Before I can answer, Nichole walks up to us, "Did you find what you were looking for?"

"We sure did!" Olivia says with wide eyes, "We found out more about Dancing Mary, too!"

Natalie tilts her head, "Who?"

I quickly stand up and motion to Olivia to do the same. "Thanks for your help, Natalie. We appreciate it."

I shuffle Olivia out of the library before she decides to divulge anymore information about Mary, Cotton or worse, the ghosts that are haunting us at the cabin. The last thing I need is the cops banging on the door in the middle of the night conducting a wellness check.

* * *

The rest of the afternoon goes without incident and other than Olivia making plans to see her grandmother and go through her mothers old pictures, there are no interruptions in what has shaped up to be a calm day. Though, with every hour the clock ticks toward night fall, I can feel a sense of anxiety rise in me hoping and praying that the strange spirits that visited us before will return. I can tell Olivia is thinking the same thing by the way she keeps checking the clock every time she walks into the kitchen. Though, both of us pretend that everything is fine. I guess we're likeminded in hoping that if we pretend that things are normal, they will be.

At dinnertime, I ask Olivia what she feels like eating just as her phone rings. After a few brief moments on the phone, Olivia tells me that her grandmother would like to see her tonight instead of tomorrow and surprisingly is willing to let Winston go along too.

"Can I go, Dad? Grandma said that some of mom's cousins will be going there tonight and I can finally meet them."

"Of course. Just make sure that you don't leave there without me knowing."

"My days of running off without telling you are long gone. I promise." She walks over and wraps her hands around my neck and kisses me on the cheek.

"Why has Greta agreed to letting Winston go over there. I thought she hated the thought of having a "dirty beast" in her house.

Olivia shrugs. I asked her why she changed her mind and all she said was that one of mom's cousins has two poodles and they will be bringing them to her place, so I guess that's why she said it was okay for Winston to go."

"A very complex woman, your grandmother is."

Olivia giggles, "Tell me about it."

Olivia heads to her room to get ready and stops outside of her bedroom door. Looking back at me she says, "Oh. I almost forgot. Grandma needs you to drop me off."

"Of course she does," I mutter under my breath.

* * *

We drive along the narrow, winding pavement of Back Road, which by the uneven pavement and the sporadic potholes hasn't been fixed in years, if ever. As we round a hairpin corner, Olivia tilts her head and looks up at the sky through the windshield, "It's a full moon tonight, a weird one."

Once we've rounded the sharp corner, I look out of the window and up at the sky. The moon is full but instead of having a white glowing rim around it, it's surrounded by a muddy charcoal grey ring, how strange.

I've never been to Greta's house and as we pull down a freshly paved long driveway, I half expect it to lead to a small cottage with a thatched roof, kind of like the witches house in the Hansel and Gretel storybook. Instead, we pull up to a two-level white house with a manicured front yard surrounded by a pristine white fence. Olivia hops out with Winston and tells me that she'll call me in the morning when she's ready to come home.

I watch as my teenage daughter and her dog happily sprint to the front door. My mind suddenly shifts to Laura. What would she think of our daughter spending time with the woman who was more of an opponent to her than a mother. I sigh and then slowly back out of the driveway.

Once back on the road, I glance up at the strange moon and wonder once again about the strange grey ring.

* * *

With Olivia at her grandmothers, the cabin is completely silent, enough so that I can hear the sound of waves breaking on the shore. After reading for a few hours I decide to lay on the sofa and relax my eyes, but it doesn't take long before my mind fills will snapshots of the evil red spirit and the strange things that have occurred while staying at the cabin. After a few moments of unsuccessfully trying to clear my mind , I decide to go for a walk on the beach in hopes that it will help me clear my thoughts. It's 10:30 when I glance at the clock before walking out the front door.

As soon as I'm outdoors in the cleansing sea air, my mind stops racing and I begin to relax. I make my way to the shoreline and look out over the inlet at the water. A mild wind paints the tops of small swells with a brush of white as the full moon shines dimly from above. Maybe there's a reason the moon looks so different tonight. Maybe it's the time of year, or because of the lunar cycle, or something I have no idea about. Back in the city, there's a lot of overcast and rain in the Fall, and even when there are clear nights when there is a full moon, I don't remember going outside to study the size or shape. That being said, over the years I have seen my share of moons and I can't remember any of them looking like the one that is out tonight. This moon reminds me of one that would be in a thriller movie where there's an eerie setting like an old castle or house and up above, to create an element of suspense, there would be a moon as ominous as this one.

I spend some time walking along the shore, getting close enough to where the water ebbs and flows with seafoam bubbling about a foot away from where I'm strolling. I can't help but think about Mary and all of the strange things she's said. I'd like to convince myself that she's completely nuts, and for a few nights after speaking with her, I thought that was the case. But at the cabin, she was genuinely concerned for the safety of Olivia and me. As far as what Olivia thinks, about Mary being the same woman who was killed by her husband in the mid 1800s, I highly doubt it. I can't explain the orb like creatures who have been frequenting the cabin, but there's no way Mary is a ghost. I have reached out and touched her before, she's as alive and as real as I am. Thinking as I walk, I barely realize how far I've gone up the beach until I see the lights from the Comox Marina ahead. With a cooler wind starting off the ocean, I decide to turn back and make my way along the shore towards home.

As I amble along, a large gull swoops down and lands a few feet from me to wade along the shallows peering into the water for a late-night snack. This is a beautiful area of the Coast. I only wish that Laura was still alive and we could've taken this trip together. But life had other plans for us. I only hope that wherever she is, in heaven, or dancing among the stars that her soul is free and she has finally found peace.

As I near the area of the beach in front of the cabin, I turn from the sea and am just making my way toward home when I see a flash of light out of the corner of my eye. I turn and notice Mary, she's wearing a white flowy cloak, or maybe a gown. I raise my hand to wave hello and she immediately stops as though she's just noticed me. Then, she quickly turns and heads toward the dense forest at the end of the beach. I call out loudly against the wind hoping that she'll hear me but, she is either ignoring me or she doesn't hear me. I wonder why she is wearing what could be a housecoat or a nightgown. Is she okay? I decide to follow her just in case there's something wrong.

Chapter Thirteen

An eerie fog covers the forest floor as I do my best to walk undetected across the sand until I reach the edge of the thicket. The trail is narrow with roots and ferns making it barely visible. Still, I do my best to stay on the path and follow Mary's footsteps. The occasional glimmer of moonlight bursts through the thick canvas of treetops overhead, temporarily offering a glimpse of Mary moving effortlessly through the dense forest. Staying far enough behind so that she doesn't hear me, I strain to focus on each direction she moves. After what seems like an hour, the trees give way to a small clearing. I move as close as possible to the spot where Mary has stopped in the middle of a grassy span. Mary kneels and the fog fades away. Her white cloak with her long dark hair under the moonlight give her an other worldly appearance. I watch intently as she begins pawing at the ground, pulling up grass and then digging into the dirt, which colors the front of her white smock a dark brown. What the hell is she doing? Is she mimicking an animal and performing some strange ritual under the moon?

Digging vigorously, Mary pulls at the earth until piles of dirt have formed around her. I stare at this strange spectacle, frozen in place, needing to know what she is up to. After a few long moments, she stops and straightens her back, looking into the shallow hole she's created. Then, she raises her soil covered hands to the night sky and begins to sing. At first her voice is intrusive, as it breaks through the silence of the forest but then I hear the rhythm, a beautiful song that dances through the trees. I try to make out the words but it soon becomes obvious that she's singing in another language, one

I've never heard before. Mary lowers her gaze back to the hole in front of her and then dips both hands into the hole. Grasping handfuls of something white and small in size, Mary brings her finds to her chest and rocks back and forth, still singing the beautiful song.

I feel my foot beginning to slip down the exposed root of the tree I am standing on and try to regain my footing, but it's too late. My foot slips and I fall backward, landing on a stack of broken tree branches. I jump to my feet and look ahead to where Mary was sitting, but she's gone. The sound of my weight against the rotten branches must've startled her. I scan the area, looking for a glimpse of her white gown but all I see are trees and darkness. Just in case she returns to the clearing, I wait and watch for a long time. When I realize she won't be returning, I make my way to the hole she was making in the middle of the clearing. As I approach, I notice the small white items that Mary was holding strewn among the freshly unearthed soil. I bend down and grab onto one of them, and after brushing off the dirt and turning it over, I realize that it's a small shell and there are many just like it inside that shallow pit Mary dug. How curious. Why would she be digging up a pit full of shells, and more importantly, who buried all of them in the first place? Then, I remember that the online book Olivia and I were reading at the library mentioned the K'ómoks people and how they would find beautiful shells and bury them in the ground in special plots.

* * *

It was a harder walk leaving the forest than entering it, with sharp sticks jabbing into my ankles along the rustic path. By the time I reach home, my mind is full with questions about Mary and what I saw her doing in the woods. I wonder where she lives and if she has people who care about her nearby. Momentarily forgetting about the red spirit who could make another unwelcomed appearance, I take a hot shower to wash the blood from my ankles.

Once I've dried off and gotten into my pajamas, I go to the kitchen and pour myself a stiff drink. Exhausted from my trek through the tangled woods, it doesn't take long before the alcohol helps to sedate me and I drift off to sleep.

* * *

The ringing of my phone jolts me awake. I reach over and grab it from the side table. Clearing my throat, I answer.

"Dad. Thank God you're okay. You scared the heck out of me. I've been calling you since 9 am." Olivia says excitedly.

Confused, I rub my eyes and glance up at the clock, it's almost noon. I quickly sit up.

"Is everything alright?" I ask.

"Yes. Now that you've finally answered. Were you sleeping this whole time?"

"Unbelievably, I guess I was. I never sleep that long. I guess I must've needed it."

"Well, now that you're awake, do you think you can come and get Winston and me?"

I tell her to give me a few minutes to change and I'll be on my way.

* * *

Greta stands in the doorway as I pull up to the house. She is wearing a bright caftan and the same scowl on her face that she always has. I give a quick wave but she doesn't lower herself to return the greeting. Olivia and Winston come around the side of the house, and after a quick goodbye to her grandmother, both dog and child are in the car and we're driving away.

"So, how was your night?" I ask.

Olivia shrugs, "Okay I guess. Other than grandma having a melt down over Winston jumping on her bed with dirty paws, nothing really bad happened."

I look at Winston in the mirror and smile, I like him even more now.

Olivia tells me about meeting some of her mother's extended family. She tells me that they were nice enough but definitely different personalities than her mom had. I'm not surprised. From what Laura told me; her family was always judgemental and snobby.

"Did you see anything spooky at the cabin last night, dad?"

"Nope. It was all good."

"Are you sure? If something did happen, you should tell me." She persists.

"Okay. Okay. You got me. The ghosts did return around midnight."

Olivia's eyes widen, "And?"

"And I told them they could hang around for awhile if they promised to do the laundry and clean up that awful space you call a bedroom."

She crosses her arms and slumps back in the seat, "Very funny, Dad."

After a few moments, she says, "You know what? I'm not surprised at all that the ghosts didn't return last night. I bet if I would've stayed home last night, they would've showed up, at least the evil red one would've."

"Let's not think like that, Olivia. Let's not give this whole thing more power and attention. I know it's strange and scary but it's important to remember that if they are in fact ghosts, they can't hurt us. We are alive and real and they are not."

"Nice speech, Dad, but they sure seem real when they're flying at you."

She's got a point but I don't want to fuel the situation so I change the subject and suggest we pick up breakfast and head back home.

As we drive down Comox Ave, the sun breaks through the clouds and illuminates the landscape. "It's really pretty here, dontcha think, Dad? It's hard to believe that mom would ever want to leave such a nice little town.

I explain to her that her mother had her own reasons for leaving Comox.

"Yeah, I know. Grandma told me. She said that Mom didn't believe in God and because of that, grandma told her that if she was going to be an atheist, she had no place in the family."

"That's bullshit!" I yell, accidentally stepping on the brakes.

Both Olivia and Winston lunge forward. "Geez Dad, chill out. I didn't say that I believed her. Sheesh."

I take a deep breath then exhale slowly, composing myself. "I'm sorry, Olivia. I shouldn't have reacted that way."

"You've really gotta mellow out, Dad."

"Yes. I know. It's just that your grandmother has a way of getting under my skin."

"So, why is it that grandma thought Mom didn't believe in God? Maybe she didn't. That would explain why I never grew up going to church."

I shake my head, "Going to church has very little to do with believing in God, and just for the record, your mom used to read the bible regularly and she was definitely a Christian."

"Hmm. That's interesting. If that's true, maybe she would have been able to pray or say a verse out of the bible that could've chased that horrible red spirit away. Then again, if Mom hadn't died we never would've come to Comox and we never would've seen that ghost in the first place."

"Your analysis is dizzying, Olivia."

We arrive at Tidal Café, and the three of us hop out of the car. Luckily, the sun is shining, and the patio looks open, so we head toward one of the half-dozen tables where we can bring Winston, something that wouldn't be an option in our Vancouver eateries.

Once seated, I let Olivia order for us while I pet the dog and gaze out over the sparkling inlet, replaying what she had said in the car. As silly and immature as she can be, her comment about using Bible verses to ward off evil has me thinking. Then again, Pastor Paul, whom I met at the Courtenay church, didn't seem convinced there was an easy fix for expelling bad spirits. He only suggested a prayer meeting with some of the congregation.

If we do have another encounter with the ghosts, maybe I should give him a call and try to organize something—it's not like we have anything to lose. I just hope Mary wasn't right when she said that if we leave the cabin, the evil spirit will follow us... or, more troubling, follow Olivia.

"The waitresses here are so nice, not like in the city. Our waitress gave me this for

Winston." Olivia walks up to the table, showing me the dog treat in her hand.

After breakfast, Olivia, the dog, and I head to The Spit for a walk along the long stretch of sandy beach. On the way back, I pull into the mall and wait in the car while Olivia goes inside for snacks. Thirty minutes later, she returns with two huge bags of junk food and a puzzle.

* * *

The living room floor has been transformed into a carpet party with candy wrappers, chip bags and soda cans strewn everywhere. Olivia lays in amongst the debris constructing her new puzzle as I lay on the couch with Winston.

"Are you hungry for dinner, garbage guts?" I ask.

Olivia laughs "No way. I'm so full I could burst."

I'm not in any mad rush to eat either, our brunch at Tidal café' filled me up which is good because I seriously lack the energy or motivation to venture out just to get some food.

Time ticks past and before I know it the clock reads 11 pm. I suggest that Olivia should think about having a shower and then calling it a night. After hemming and hawing, she gets up to head down the hall before I point out the huge pile of junk food debris she has left on the carpet.

In true teenager form, Olivia does a half-assed job of cleaning up, leaving me the task of picking up everything she's missed.

While Olivia is in the shower, I take Winston out to pee and then make my way to my room to get ready for bed. I hear the bathroom door open in the hallway and a few seconds later, the sound of Olivia's door closing. After getting into bed, I reach out and shut off the lamp on the side table and lay my head back on the pillow and am just closing my eyes when I see a dull glow coming from the wall that separates Olivia's room from mine. I sit up in the darkness and stare at the quickly expanding glow. At first, it appears to be a yellow color but then I quickly notice more and more red appear in the center. I don't need to sit here to try and figure out what this spot is and what's going to happen next. I jump to my feet and race down the hallway to Olivia's room.

"Dad. Seriously?" Olivia's is standing in her housecoat with her pajama's laid out in front of her on the bed. "I was just about to get changed. If you had come in even one second later, both you and I could've been emotionally scarred for life."

Ignoring her words, I take a deep breath and try to speak calmly so as not to upset her. "Is there any chance you could call your grandmother to pick you up?"

"What? Are you kidding? Look at the time, Dad. Grandma is older than dirt and old people go to bed really early. Why do you want me to call her?”

“I umm. I just think it’s a good idea is all.”

“Lame reason, Dad. What’s really going on?”

“You ask too many questions. All I need you to do is to dial your grandma and ask if you can stay the night. If she can’t come and get you, I can drive you.”

Olivia folds her arms in front of her and pushes her shoulders back, the same stance she always takes when she’s in defiance mode. “I’m not doing anything until you tell me what’s going on.”

We stand and stare silently at each other for the next fer moments until she suddenly cocks her head and nods. “I know what this is about. You saw something didn’t you?”

I stay silent locked in her gaze.

“You saw that evil ghost, didn’t you?”

I sigh audibly.

"Dad! Smarten up! You want me to be honest with you and yet you wont tell me the truth."

She's right. As much as I'm trying to keep her from getting scared, I can't expect her to be honest with me if I'm lying to her.

"No. I did not see the evil spirit, only a hint of it on the wall."

Olivia's eyes widen and the blood quickly drains from her face. "Oh no."

Seeing the fear in her, I quickly try to diffuse the situation. "Maybe what I saw was a passing car with their headlights reflecting through the window and onto the wall."

"Nice try," she scoffs. "What color did you see?"

"Yellow, mostly. And then, a touch of red."

"Oh no. It's that evil ghost. He's back." Olivia puts her hands over her face and starts to cry. I walk over and wrap my arms around her, holding her tightly to me. "Nothing's going to happen to you. I promise."

She sniffs and chokes on her tears a couple of times then lifts her head and looks at me, "I think maybe I should call grandma."

I reach over and grab her phone from the bedside table and hand it to her. Staying close to her while she calls, I look around the room at the walls, praying that the red glowing light doesn't appear.

After a long few moments, Olivia hangs up. "She isn't answering. I knew she'd be asleep."

"That's okay. Lets just keep calm and take Winston and go to the living room."

At least if we're in the front room, we'll be closer to the front door in case something strange does happen.

Once we're on the couch, Olivia slides close to me.

"Why don't you play a game on your phone for awhile," I suggest, hoping to distract her.

With the sound muted, she opens up the game ap on her phone and starts to play Candy Crush. My eyes scan the room, specifically the walls looking for any color changes. I watch Winston as well, looking for any signs that he senses an energy approaching. So far, he looks relaxed as he nuzzles his head into Olivia's lap. After about half an hour, I'm just about to get up to get a glass of water when there's a loud bang on the door. Olivia screams and the dog barks and I jump to my feet. "Stay here," I say, my heard pounding hard inside my chest.

I walk over and approach the door, forcing myself to take air into my lungs.

"Dad. Be careful." Olivia's voice is shaky and scared.

Cautiously I reach for the handle. Once the cold knob is in my grasp, I scrunch up my eyes, and wordlessly ask the spirt world, *please don't let anything that I can't deal with be out there.*

Turning the handle bit by bit, I ready myself. When I feel a click, I pull the door open and a gust of wind forces its way into the room. I step out onto the top of the steps and look out into the cold night, nothing is there.

"What is it, Dad. Who's out there?" Olivia cries.

I turn to walk back inside when my eyes catch a glimpse of something like a large spot that's dark red in color on the side of the house. I lean in close to take a better look but I can't quite make out what is out there. I reach inside and flip on the porch light then look again. With the help of the light, I easily make out five thin fingers and a palm, a handprint. I reach over and touch it and then look at my finger. A red almost powdery substance that has a fine grit to the texture covers my fnger. Strange. Why would someone leave a red handprint on the house? It's not like it was here before now as I would've seen it while coming and going.

This is new. I look out into the darkness again, this time listening intently for sounds of someone fleeing but there's only the sound of the wind.

Back inside, Olivia stands impatiently staring at me with her eyes huge and unblinking.

"Calm down. Everything is okay. There's nobody out there." I finish closing the door and then lock it.

"Then what was that loud crashing sound?"

"Probably just the wind blowing stuff around."

Olivia's shoulders drop and she exhales loudly then slumps down on the couch and picks up her phone. "Maybe I should leave grandma a message just in case she wakes up in the night to go to the bathroom or something."

She begins to punch in Greta's number just as the phone rings.

Olivia looks at the phone, "It's her!"

After a few moments of Olivia pleading for her grandmother to come and get her, she finally ends the call and smiles. "Okay, she said she's on her way."

I sigh. "I'm sure she's really pleased about having to come all the way over here so late at night. Don't expect her personality to be too sunny when you wake up in the morning."

Olivia shrugs, "I'm not worried. Besides, now that the cousins are gone, maybe tomorrow she'll finally let me take some of Mom's old photo's home." She heads off to her room to get ready. After about twenty minutes, there's a honking sound outside. I look through the window and see Greta's car in the driveway then call to Olivia to hurry up. When she appears from her room, she's in her street clothes and has her pack over one shoulder. Winston is happily beside her with his leash hooked on and his tongue hanging out, ready for adventure.

Once they reach the living room, Olivia stops in front of me, "Are you going to be okay here alone?"

I smile. "Don't worry. I'll be just fine."

"Okay. Just call me if any weird stuff happens. My phone is on and I sleep at the back of the house in the spare room so no one will hear if my phone rings."

"Okay. If I need a bodyguard, you're the first person I'll call."

Olivia shakes her head and opens the front door and leads Winston out when she suddenly stops. "Dad. Come and see this! She says, standing in the doorway.

I walk over and peek out of the door.

"It's a handprint. Can you see it?"

"Oh. Interesting. I say. Maybe some local kids were monkeying around and left that there." I don't want her to know I've already seen the print.

"You know what's weird? The last time I stayed the night at grandma's, that same red color was in the bottom of my backpack. I tried to empty it out but every time I look in it, there's more red powder stuff."

Greta honks the horn impatiently.

Olivia grabs Winston's leash, kisses me quickly on the cheek and heads to the car.

Once Greta pulls out of the driveway, I go back inside and think about the red handprint on the house and what Olivia said about the powder she found in her backpack. Something strange is going on, I just wish I knew what the hell it was.

* * *

I wake to the sound of my laptop hitting the floor and quickly sit up and inspect it for damages. Thankfully nothing appears to be broken. Olivia must've forgotten to put it away before she left and instead placed it on the bottom of the couch where my feet accidentally kicked it off. Standing up, I stretch and feel a cramp in the middle of my back, compliments of the bumpy old sofa.

After grabbing a glass of water, I walk over to the window and watch the small waves, with their slight whitecaps, gently rolling down the inlet. It looks like the wind has died down quite a bit. I spend the next half hour stretching and shifting around, trying to work out the knot in my back, but nothing seems to help. Finally, I decide that a short walk on the beach might loosen me up.

My mind is still reeling from the red glowing energy I saw earlier, not to mention the strange handprint outside. It's clear I won't be getting much sleep tonight. I slip into my street clothes, throw on my coat and shoes, and head out the door.

Chapter Fourteen

As soon as the beach comes into view, I spot someone crouched by the water's edge. There's only one person it could be. I push forward against a moderate wind, keeping my hands in my pockets for warmth.

Mary's hands are covered in what looks like red powder. She kneels on the wet sand, humming softly as she stares out over the choppy sea. Assuming she must've heard me approach, I raise my voice to be heard over the crashing waves. "Are you digging for shells?"

Obviously startled, she turns her head toward me and quickly scrambles to her feet. "Why are you here?" she asks, her voice sharp.

Taken aback, I take a moment to find an answer. "I saw you from the cabin window and I thought I would come and speak to you. I have questions."

She steps closer, "About what?"

"About the angry spirit that appears when Olivia is in the cabin. Thomas Cotton. He was your husband, wasn't he? He did something awful to you many years ago. Is that right?"

Mary looks down and finally nods her head.

"But you're real. I don't understand. How could you be flesh and bone, and a ghost at the same time?"

Slowly Mary raises her eyes to mine. "I'm not sure. All I know is that until you and your daughter arrived at the cabin, I was not in my body. For well over a century, I have existed as an energy, floating over the land, lost and alone. This form I am in is the same body I had before Thomas Cotton wrapped his hands around my throat and ended my

243

life. When I need to, I can leave this body and take my spirit form.”

“This all seems so surreal. My logical mind tells me that everything you’re saying is impossible, but after repeatedly witnessing the haunting visits, I guess logic has kind of flown out the window.” Even though I think I know the answer, I need to hear the words from her mouth. “Are you the blue spirit who shows up when the evil red energy comes after Olivia?”

Mary nods then reaches out with her cold red hands and grasps my arm, “We need to find Thomas Cotton. That’s the only way.”

I shake my head, “Wait. What do you mean find him? How? He lived many years ago.”

“His bones.”

“You want to dig up his bones? What good will that do. Is there a ritual using his bones that will send his spirit away?”

Mary nods while keeping her eyes locked on mine.

"But, how the hell are we supposed to know where to look for his bones? Was he buried in a graveyard at least?"

"No. He is buried where he died. I'm not sure where. He ate special berries that were left for him to find. He ate them and then fell to the ground."

"Who left the berries? Was it you?"

She shakes her head. "I was long gone by then. I've never known who sent him to the spirit world, I think it may have been my family but I can't be sure. The villagers found him and buried him in the ground in an unmarked grave. I stood nearby and watched."

"Where was he buried?"

Mary raises her hand and points behind me, "There."

I turn and look to where she's pointing. "In the forest? He was buried in the forest?"

She nods.

"Is that why you were digging a hole the other night when I followed you? You were looking for his bones?"

Mary nods. "Yes, I buried shells near his body so I would know where he was, only, there are so many holes with shells, and no matter how hard I've searched, I can't find his bones. I need your help. I need you to help me find him so I can separate his spirit from this world, and away from your daughter. It's the only way."

A barking sound in the distance causes me to turn toward the cabin. I'm shocked to see Winston running toward me with Olivia close behind.

I turn to look back at Mary but she's gone. I look both ways on the beach but she's nowhere to be seen.

"Dad. Catch him. He's gone mental."

Winston runs up and jumps on me, his paws leaving wet sand all over my pants. Olivia reaches us, panting and bending over to catch her breath. The cabin door was locked and the car was there so I thought you might be out here."

"I thought your grandma was dropping you off in the afternoon?"

Olivia shrugs, "So did I but she changed her mind after Winston crapped on her white carpet."

I smile and pat the dog on the head. "Good boy."

Chapter Fifteen

The sun has been sporadically breaking through gaps in the clouds, and aside from the occasional sprinkle, it's been a fairly pleasant day. I went out briefly this morning to grab some fresh fruit and cereal, which helped distract me from the chaos of thoughts swirling in my head. But now that I'm back home, there's nothing to pull my attention away from Mary's words about Cotton and the unsettling statements she made about finding his bones. They drift uneasily through my mind, making it impossible to focus on anything else. Thankfully, Olivia is preoccupied with a movie on my laptop, so I don't have to be fully present. Greta will be away for the next couple of days, from what Olivia said, she's going to Victoria for a church ladies get-a-way. So much for Olivia getting her mothers pictures until she gets back. I could swear that Greta has been delaying giving Laura's photos to Olivia in some sort of bid to assert her control, something the old woman is very good at. Unfortunately, Olivia is young and tends to take people at face value. There's no point in me saying anything to her, she would only get defensive and tell me that I'm jumping to conclusions.

Daylight merges quickly into night and after eating take-out food and having a laid-back evening, it's time for bed. Olivia spends a half hour with Winston outside, walking around the lighted streets and giving him some exercise so he sleeps through the night. When they return, I'm in my pajamas and have all but the hallway light turned off.

"Do you thing we'll have any creepy visitors tonight?"

"Probably not. And if anything strange appears remember that it can't hurt you."

"Yeah. Sure! That's not an easy thing to remember when an evil ghost is only inches from your face."

"I'm sure nothing is going to happen but if you get scared, I'm in the next room. Besides, you have Winston. He's your bodyguard and I know he won't let anything bad happen to you."

"Yeah. I actually do feel a lot safer since we got him."

With my head on the pillow, I can't help but reflect on Olivia's fears about getting another unwanted visit from that demon-like spirit. Thankfully, the wall separating Olivia's room and mine looks normal and there's no sign of the red hue. Still, like my daughter, I don't want to see the ghost either. I reach over on the nightstand and turn the lamp on. I have seen the spirit a few times, but usually when the lights are off and it's dark, never in a lit up room. I grab my phone, also on the table and text Olvia good night and then suggest that in order for her to feel a bit safer, she too should leave a light on.

* * *

The unmistakable sound of shattering glass is followed by Winston's shrill, panicked barking. My heart skips a beat. I leap out of bed, sprinting down the hallway and throwing open Olivia's door. Winston is frantic, jumping from the bed to the floor, then back to me at the doorway, his barking relentless. I can't see Olivia anywhere so I step forward and look between the broken window and the bed. Olivia is surrounded by what looks like thousands of pieces of broken glass. As soon as she see's me, she lets out a faint, desperate cry. "Daddy. He came back. I couldn't scream. I tried so hard. And Winston couldn't even bark."

"Just don't move. I'll come and get you," I say, trying to steady my breath.

I rush to the front room, half-sliding into my shoes before darting back to Olivia. When I reach her, I carefully lift her into my arms, my pulse racing as I try to make sense of the chaos.

It's when I set her down on the bed that I notice all of the little cuts and scrapes on her legs and arms, one of the cuts seems to be bleeding quite badly.

"I thought you said that the red ghost couldn't hurt me but you were wrong. He did hurt me, Dad." She continues sobbing.

I'm in complete shock but I know I have to put everything out of my head so I can concentrate on her wounds. I tell her to sit still then sprint to the bathroom searching for any gauze, bandages or antiseptic. When I return to her room, I place a box of band aids and some cotton swabs on the bed—the only wound care items I could find. As I dab the cotton on her skin to clean up some of the blood, I'm relieved to see that most of her wounds are superficial and small. However, the gash on her ankle is still bleeding quite a lot.

"It stings like crazy."

I press on the ankle wound with the cotton and keep the pressure on for a few minutes, but when I lift the swab, blood is still trickling out. I'm no doctor but my best guess is that she needs a stitch or two. I give her the swab and tell her to hold it firmly on her ankle then I quickly go to my room, get dressed and return with my housecoat for Olivia. Once I have the robe around her, I carry her out to the car and sit her on the passenger seat.

"Dad. Don't leave Winston here alone. The window in my room is busted and anyone could get in and take him or hurt him."

After I let the dog into the backseat, I rush back into the house and grab my wallet and then shut the front door.

On the drive to the hospital, I tell Olivia to try and remember everything she can about what happened.

"If it wasn't for Mary, I might be dead right now." She sniffs back tears.

"Mary? What do you mean?"

"She is the blue light. When that evil red spirit came into my room, he was hovering over me with his mouth open. That's when I first tried to scream but couldn't. I think he was trying to suck my soul out of my body, I really do."

I shake my head, not because I don't believe she's telling me the truth but because it's all so confusing and surreal.

"Then, out of nowhere, Mary rushed through the air and hit the red ghost. He forced her into the corner and then came back and picked me up. I didn't know what he was planning on doing to me but I knew it was going to be very bad. And all I could think about was that I'd never see you again." Olivia covers her face with her hands and sobs.

I rub her back and tell her everything is going to be okay now.

Olivia wipes her nose on the back of her hands, "Mary saved my life, Dad. She kept coming at him and then finally, he threw me against the window and then went after her. They were swirling above me and all around the room."

"Tell me why you think it was Mary that helped you. What makes you believe she is the blue energy?"

Olivia scowls at me, "Dad. It's her. Like I said before, she is Dancing Mary."

* * *

The florescent lights are blinding as we enter the emergency ward of the hospital. Just before I carried Olivia from the car, I told her that we should refrain from telling the medical staff about what really happened and how she got injured. She came up with a great alternative to the truth, she was playing with Winston and accidentally threw a baseball through the window. I'm just hoping that the doctor doesn't question it, otherwise they'll probably call the police and want to investigate. If that happens and they question my ability to care for my daughter safely, they could take her away from me. I don't know what I'd do if that was the case. Olivia is my whole world and more importantly, I'm all she has.

The intake nurse gets all of Olivia's information then directs us to a cot in the triage area where they hand Olivia a hospital gown and ask her to change. "You can wait outside," she says to me before the nurse pulls the curtain closed. In front of the curtain, I pace back and forth, not only because I'm worried about Olivia's wounds and how bad they may be but also because of the frightening incident that brought us here. Then there's Olivia's claims of Mary and how she is convinced it was Mary that saved her, in her ghost form. It's all too much for my head to process.

A doctor walks up to the nursing station and a nurse hands him a clipboard before he makes his way over to me. He asks me what happened to bring us into emergency and I tell him the honest bits first, how I hear a loud noise coming from my daughter's room and how when I got there, I found her against the wall and under the broken window. I left out all of the surreal parts, that we have an evil ghost that's stalking us and how Olivia was rescued by a good spirit named Dancing Mary which if I had said it out loud, would've undoubtedly landed me in either a jail cell or the psych ward and Olivia in a foster home.

After speaking with me, the doctor waits until the nurse draws the curtain back and then walks up beside the bed to assess Olivia's wounds. Once he's looked her over, he tells her that only the one wound, the one

I was most concerned about will need four or five sutures. Olivia looks at me with little girl eyes and whines, "I'm scared."

I walk up beside the bed and rub her back gently, something I used to do when she was a small child to calm her down. "I wish mom was here. No offence, Dad. It's just that Mom was so good at stuff like this."

I'm not at all offended. She's right. Laura was a great mother and because of the long hours I put in at the firm, she dealt with 90% of Olivia's needs, from scraped knees to getting her period, Laura was always fixing things.

After a few protests from Olivia, especially over the needle used to freeze the wound, the doctor asks her if she's had a tetanus shot before. I'm just about to answer no, when Olivia pipes up, "Yeah. I had one about two years ago when I stepped on a piece of glass on the beach, something I had no knowledge of or if I did, I was probably so tired from putting in long days at work that I didn't retain it.

Once Olivia is changed back into her nighty with my housecoat overtop, they give us a small pack of fresh bandages and we are free to go.

"Dad. That sucked!" Olivia says as she reaches into the backseat and pets Winston. "I think I'm gonna sleep with you until we leave."

"I think that's the best idea."

We pull up to the house and I open the back door so Winston can pee. Olivia gets out of the passenger side and assures me that she doesn't need any help walking. As we make our way to the door, Olivia points to the side of the house, "Look, Dad. That wasn't here before."

I look to where she's pointing and see a small old shovel leaning against the house. My mind immediately goes to Mary and what she said about finding Thomas Cotton's bones.

"I wonder who put that there?" Olivia says.

I sigh, "I'm not sure."

Olivia stops and looks into my eyes, "You know, don't you? I can always tell when you're not telling me something by the way you sigh when I ask a question."

"It's chilly out here and you're in pajamas, let's go in." I say, temporarily stalling my response.

Once inside, Winston devours what's left in his food dish as I comb the cabin for something to cover the broken window in Olivia's room.

"Want my help, Dad?"

"No. I'm pretty sure you've had your share of injuries tonight. Sit on the couch and I'll do it."

Thankfully, there's a folded-up cardboard box in the hall closet that I can use. I know that I should probably be reaching out to the owner to tell him about the broken window but the last thing I want is him spending time here considering what's been going on. Not to mention Winston. I never let the owner know that we had adopted a dog.

Taping the cardboard over the window while Olivia leans in the doorway. "Are ya gonna tell me about the shovel or not?" she says.

"If I told you what I'm thinking about how the shovel got here, it's going to sound really strange." I say, sticking the final piece of tape on the window.

"Like what we've been through already isn't strange? I'm pretty sure whatever you are gonna say won't surprise me."

She has a point.

I tell Olivia to go to the living room while I sweep up the shattered glass. Once I'm finished, I get us both a glass of water from the kitchen and then I join her on the couch.

"Are you sure you want to know?" I say, handing her a glass.

She nods.

I tell her all about my last meeting on the beach with Mary and how she told me about Thomas Cotton, her ex-husband and that he died in the mid 1800s and was buried somewhere in the vicinity. "Mary said that she needs his bones so she can make him go away."

At first Olivia doesn't say anything, she just freezes like a statue with her eyes locked on mine. "I know, it sounds completely mad, doesn't it?"

She shakes her head. "Nope. It sounds believable to me. Don't forget how I accidentally conjured Thomas Cotton's ghost in the first place. If Mary says that she needs his bones, I believe her. Is that who left the shovel here?"

I nod. "I think so."

"So, she needs our help."

I nod.

"Then, that's what we'll do. We owe her that much, especially after she saved me tonight."

"Are you tired?" I ask.

"I'm exhausted, Dad. Maybe we should get some sleep before the sun comes up."

On the way down the hall, Olivia tells me that after we wake up, we should go and get supplies like a couple of flashlights and some other things that will help us to search for Cotton's grave. Hearing her say the words out loud I get a shudder up my back. I'm not sure why but something tells me that our journey is just beginning and there will be a level of danger involved.

* * *

Winston's muzzle is an inch away from my face when I open my eyes. Olivia is on the other side of me, curled up to my back. I shift my legs and immediately, the dog's eyes open. He sits up and whines, no doubt he has to go outside. I rise slowly so as not to wake Olivia, but my efforts are futile as Winston jumps behind me and licks Olivia's face. Her eyes open and in a croaky voice she laughs and pets the dog. It's incredible how strongly her feelings are for the animal considering that we haven't had him very long. Truth be told, he's growing on me too. Not to mention the fact that I owe him gratitude for helping Olivia and me to reconnect.

Olivia tells me that she will let Winston out while I get up to have a quick shower. By the time I'm showered and shaved, Olivia is in the kitchen getting a bowl of cereal. "Dad. I've got a great plan for our day." She says, with her mouth half-full.

"Olivia, seriously. I really don't need to see the half-eaten food in your mouth."

"Sorry." She answers, still chewing.

I shake my head and start to make a cup of instant coffee.

Just as the kettle boils, Olivia walks up to the sink and rinses her bowl. "Don't you want to know about my plan for us this morning."

"Yes, but first, did you let Winston out?"

"Yes. Of course, Dad. I take very good care of him."

I stir the boiling water into my cup and then walk over and sit on the sofa. "What's your plan?"

Olivia sits down beside me and says, "I think we should go to the museum in Courtenay."

I raise my eyebrows, "I never thought you were into history."

"I'm not, but I bet you anything they'll have old maps of Comox and what it looked like in the 1800s."

"For what reason?"

"So, we can try and figure out where the European's settled while they were here. And once we know that, maybe we can get a better idea of where that horrible man, Thomas Cotton is buried."

I guess the time has come for me to accept how crazy our situation is and stop trying to rationalize everything. "That's a really good idea you thought of. I'm impressed."

Olivia smiles proudly. "And after we go there, we can find a hardware store and buy the stuff we're going to need to dig him up."

"That sounds so morbid."

"True. But it is what it is."

I smirk. That's the same thing Laura used to say when she was coming to conclusions about things, "it is what it is."

Chapter Sixteen

The museum is not what I was expecting for a small town. As soon as we walk in, everywhere we look we see displays of prehistoric fossil bones, illustrations of massive sea creatures and boxes containing huge shells. There is also an extensive collection of historical black and white photos of the Comox Valley and the people who lived here so long ago.

A kindly lady about fifty walks up to Olivia and I. "Is this your first time visiting the museum?" she asks.

Olivia nods and then gets right to the point. "Do you have any maps or information on Comox Road during the time of the first settlers?"

The woman asks what years we are most interested in and once she has the information, she leads us over to a large counter with a computer. After taking a few moments to search for our request, she opens a file and turns the screen so we can see the large black and white illustrated image of what looks like a map of Comox. Olivia asks the woman for a copy of the map and after waiting a few minutes, we get the print and are on our way.

"Dad. I wonder what is making that ghost so angry." Olivia says as we're getting into the car.

"I mean, he was a murderer when he was alive, you'd think that it would be Mary who would be the angry one since he took her life."

I shrug, "I don't know the answer to that, I wish I did. What I do know is that Mary is a kindly spirit and from any book I've read about the First Nations on the coast, were not hostile people. They welcomed the settlers when they landed and went about their lives as they had done for thousands of years.”

Olivia sighs, “I guess they didn’t expect things to end up the way they did, huh?”

“I think you’re right. It’s terrible the way they were treated, their land was taken from them and they were treated like savages when in reality, they should have been respected and honored. After all, the settlers were guests to the First Nation peoples’ land.”

“Now things are a big mess, huh, Dad?”

I nod, “Yes. Unfortunately, you’re right. Indigenous people across our country are still having to fight for their rights and for their land.”

“I think that instead of being landed terrorists, the settlers should have taken lessons from the Indigenous people about how to live off the land and respect nature. Maybe then the environment wouldn’t be in such bad shape.”

I smile, "you're pretty smart for a kid."

We pull up to Midland Tools and get out of the car. "Okay, Dad. I know exactly what we'll need. I made a list in my phone so just trust me!"

"Yikes!" I laugh.

As soon as we walk into the building, we stand and look around the clean, well stocked store. Almost immediately, an employee approaches and asks us if he can assist us with anything. The service, plus the aesthetics of the store are already miles above anything you would find at an independent supply shop in the city. After the clerk helps us find every item on Olivia's list, a shovel, two flashlights, large garbage bags and gardening gloves, we're at the till and ready to pay.

"People sure are nice in this store. It's so different from shopping in Vancouver, isn't it?"

I nod. "Yes, I can definitely see the appeal of the Comox Valley and why so many people come here to retire."

"If you didn't have your firm back home, would you ever move to a small town like this one?"

I think for a moment, "I think I would. But there's no sense thinking about that, not when you're not yet out of high school. Besides, I don't think the people at the firm would appreciate it too much if I just walked away and left them without jobs."

"But maybe one day you'll think about moving to a place like this?"

"Only if your grandma moves away from here. Then, maybe I'd consider it." I grin.

"Not funny, Dad."

* * *

Night comes quickly and other than a few scattered clouds, the sky is clear and starry.

"This is perfect weather for our search," Olivia says looking out the living room window." Her voice is energetic and excited which is a tad concerning considering the morose nature of our quest.

"I wonder if we'll see Mary in the woods. What do you think, Dad?"

"No idea." I say, stirring a pot of canned chilli on the stove.

"We definitely have to bring Winston. It's too bad we didn't have a piece of Thomas Cottons bones; we could have let Winston take a sniff and then maybe he'd be able to smell where the grave is."

"Can we not discuss human remains before dinner?" I say, spooning the food into two bowls.

After we eat, Olivia washes the dishes then sprints down the hall to get changed into appropriate clothes for our search. When she returns to the front room, I can't help but laugh, everything she's wearing is black. "Why are you dressed like that?"

She looks at her outfit and then back at me, "I'm in camouflage."

I shake my head, "Is that so you can sneak up on the grave, utilizing the element of surprise?" I snicker.

"No. It's so nobody sees me lurking around the woods at night."

"Great idea. But you're forgetting one thing."

"What?"

We'll be carrying flashlights and we have a dog with us. I think it'll be just about impossible for us to be incognito."

Olivia sighs. "Whatever."

We grab what we'll need for our trek, even though I'm almost positive our search won't yield any results. I'm sure by now, if Cotton's grave hasn't been found since he was buried in the mid 1800s, Olivia and I probably aren't going to be the ones to locate it, especially in the dark. As we head around the house to the beach, the easiest way to get to the forest, I can't help but feeling like I'm a villager in an old black and white horror movie, off to seek out Frankenstein, all I'm missing is an oil lamp and a pitchfork.

As we step onto the beach, I look around for Mary but she's nowhere in sight. Winston runs ahead of us and stops every few feet to sniff dried seaweed and other treasures that have washed in with the tide.

Once we reach the woods we stop and look at the thicket. "Where are we supposed to enter?" Olivia says, perplexed. "I don't see a path or an opening anywhere."

Then, I remember how I entered the forest when I was following Mary. I tell Olivia to follow me and I lead her around the outside edge of the trees until I see the narrow grown-over pathway.

I turn my flashlight on and Olivia follows suit as we slowly begin our way into the dark woods carrying our shovels and a bag.

"Watch your footing. There are sharp sticks and overgrowth everywhere," I say.

Winston veers off of the path and is weaving in and out of the trees next to us.

"I wonder if the grave has any markers or anything saying Thomas Cotton's name." Olivia says.

"I highly doubt it. From the look of the old map of Comox, the area was made up of dense forests, whereas now, there are lots of buildings and infrastructure. There probably aren't a lot of stones unturned in these parts. Too many people. I think this patch of woods is probably the only area left on Comox Ave that hasn't been chopped down. I'm sure after a few more years there will be apartment buildings or houses where we're walking."

"That's kind of sad, dontcha think?"

"Yes. But that's the way it is. Money rules over everything else and if developers with pockets full of cash set their sites on prime land, inevitably they will have it."

"I bet the First Nations people are pretty pissed off that the land their ancestors lived on for so many centuries has been mowed down and turned into a cement jungle."

"Yes. I bet you're right."

Suddenly, Winston stars to bark. We stop and shine our flashlights into the trees but can't see him anywhere.

"Come on, Winston." Olivia hollers. "Here Boy!"

But her words are drowned out by Winston's barking. Wherever he is, he's not moving. We'd normally hear the rustling of his body brushing past twigs and branches, but instead, there's only the sound of his barking. Whatever has his attention, it's something that's completely holding him in place. "Winston! Winston!" Olivia hollers repeatedly but to no avail.

"Should we go and look for him?" she asks anxiously.

"No. We'd never get through the dense brush. Our best bet is to stay on the path and once he gets bored looking at whatever he's cornered, he'll find us."

"But what if it's a bear or something?"

"I bet you anything he's found a skunk or a raccoon. He'll be fine."

Slowly, I trudge ahead, navigating as best I can with the flashlight. I hear Olivia slip but before I can turn to catch her, she grabs the back of my jacket and rights herself. I remind her to be careful as we continue on the path. After a few more minutes of walking, Winston's barking ceases and Olivia shouts out to him. Now able to hear her voice, we hear the dog running through the bushes toward us. Soon, Winston is behind us on the path and Olivia breathes a sigh of relief.

"Maybe we should stop and look at the map again," she suggests.

I wait until we reach a large stump on the side of the path, then stop. Olivia hands me the map, and I lay it out on the stump, both of us shining our flashlights on it.

Even though the map has little relevance to the landscape now, I can see the waterline and guess where we came into the woods. An old road on the map looks like it would've run almost through where our rental cabin is and then around these trees. Small x's mark where buildings were between the inlet and the road, so, my best guess is, when someone who lived in the settlement died, they would've been buried near to where the people lived.

"What do you think, Dad? Do you think we're in a good spot to start looking for a grave?"

I shrug. "I really don't know. I mean...considering how many years have passed and the buildings that have since been built, there's a chance that Thomas Cotton didn't live among the settlers village, he could've lived a ways away. I just don't know for sure."

Olivia sighs, "But it would make sense that if these woods are here and were when he lived, and no apartments or houses have been built here since he died, and no one has discovered his grave while they were constructing buildings or whatever, then there's a good chance he's in this area.

She has a point. But considering how thick the foliage and rotted branches are on the forest floor, finding anything resembling a grave would be near impossible.

"We've got nothing to lose so let's just keep walking."

I fold the map and hand it back to Olivia who puts it in her coat pocket and zips it up. Winston sticks fairly close to us after having a face-to-face encounter with whatever critter scared him.

After about fifteen minutes of manipulating our way over debris on the old trail, my flashlight shines on a clearing ahead, the same clearing where I saw Mary digging the pit full of shells.

Olivia sees the clearing as well, "Hey. Look. Finally, there's a flat area. Maybe we'll find some clues there."

I don't want to let on that I've been here before. Telling her about what I saw with Mary pawing a hole in the ground and then how she found the shells and sang as she held them up to her chest. Olivia would have a field day with that information and would undoubtedly ask me questions non-stop, questions I don't have the answers to.

We reach the clearing and Olivia and Winston immediately scale the perimeter. Whereas I make a beeline for where I saw Mary not long ago. Somewhat keeping an eye on my daughter, I walk over to where the pit of shells were, only there's no sign of the pit. I shine my light slowly over every inch of the space in front of me but not one shell is visible, not to mention, there's no sign of the earth being dug up either, something that would be hard to hide.

"Dad. Come here, you've got to see this."

I look across the grassy area where Olivia is slowly moving her light around the edge of the grass. I make my way over to her and ask what she's looking at.

"Do you see those plants? The big ones with the huge leaves on them?"

I take a few steps forward and focus where she's shining the light.

"Ok. I see them. What's the big deal?"

"The big deal is that they are Devil's Club plants."

I look at her and shrug. "And that means what?"

Olivia huffs, "Dad. Devil's club was and is still used by Indigenous people in ceremonies to ward off evil spirits."

"Really? So, why is it alarming that the plants are here in the forest?"

"Look closer. They've been brought here, the stems are not attached to the ground."

I shine my light into the piles of plants and see stems and roots laying on top of one another. "That is strange."

"I know. The plants are thought to be magical. It's not just the leaves that were used for protection against dark forces; the stems have a black coal like substance that the coastal First Nations used as face paint that also acted as a shield against evil."

I look at Olivia, "and how the heck do you know all of this?"

"First of all, you're forgetting how into the metaphysical stuff I was, and secondly, the question shouldn't be how I know stuff but why all of the Devil's Club is here!"

"Good point."

Winston whines and Olivia and I both turn to see him in the center of the grassy area, staring at the ground.

"What's the matter, Boy." Olivia asks, walking past me toward the dog.

I briefly shine my light back at the Devils Club then turn and follow Olivia.

Once I make it to where Olivia and Winston are standing, both staring at a pile of small white feathers.

"Do you think a bird was eaten here?"

I shake my head. "No. I don't see any limbs or blood."

I walk closer to the pile and lean down just as a gust of wind rushes through the trees. I back up and stand beside Olivia as the breeze picks up the feathers and swirls them together like a tornado.

"Whoa. This is crazy," Olivia says.

We stand motionless and watch the wind pick up every last feather until we're staring into what looks like a perfect white cylinder, twisting before us. Winston whines as the newly formed tornado starts to shift across the grass. At first, the twister moves to the right, to where the grass ends and the trees begin, before shifting direction and traveling to the left. The three of us are transfixed, frozen where we stand as this peculiar phenomenon unfolds.

"Look. It's not travelling anymore; it's just spinning in one spot." Olivia exclaims. "I wonder why? Can we go and check it out?"

she asks. "I don't think it'll hurt us dad, after all it's just feathers."

Throughout my life when I was confronted with situations that may not have been safe, I always had a feeling in my gut that made me back off, but right now, I don't have that feeling. Olivia is right, the little tornado is made up of soft little feathers, what's the worse that could happen?

I nod and tell Olivia that I'll lead the way. We walk across the grass to where the twister is and I grab onto Olivia's hand as we walk to the edge of the grass.

"It's still not moving." Olivia says as we continue on to the other side of the twisting feathers.

When we're close enough, about arms length from the white cylinder, Winston surprises us both by darting at the feathers. Then in a flash, the twister spins high up, as high as the tree tops. And as if it was a firecracker, the twister explodes into a massive white cloud. One by one the feathers float to earth, covering the grassy area in a pale fluffy blanket.

Olivia drops the bag along with her shovel and runs into the middle of the clearing spinning around and kicking up feathers with her feet. "It's like snow, Dad. Isn't it beautiful?"

Winston romps through the whiteness, catching the feathers in his mouth. I stand and watch, barely believing what we just saw. I catch myself smiling at the playfulness of both my child and her dog. But after a few moments, I feel a strange energy come over me which diminishes the joy I was just feeling. Something makes me turn around and look behind me into the dark woods. I spot a glowing red hue speeding through the trees and heading towards us. "Olivia!" I holler, get over here now.

Her laughter stops, and she calls out "Why? This is fun."

"Now!" I say, not taking my eyes off of the red energy getting closer and closer and growing in size.

I hear the dog and Olivia as they walk over to me. "Take my hand." I tell her, dropping my shovel.

"Dad. Are you losing it? What's the matter?"

Winston starts to bark and back up, and finally, Olivia see's the red light.

"Oh no. He's back. He found us. I'm so scared, Dad."

"Just stand close to me and don't move."
Her hand shakes in mine.

The energy shifts as the red glow continues to grow brighter, casting an eerie light across the clearing. The sound of Winston's frantic barking fills the air, the tension quickly escalating. Olivia presses herself closer to me, I sense her fear now matching mine.

"Dad, it's Thomas Cotton. He's come to get me." she cries, her voice trembling.

I try to stay calm, despite the dread building in my chest.

"Stay close," I say again, my voice low but firm. The hairs on the back of my neck stand on end. "Whatever happens, don't let go of me."

The red light is almost upon us now, and I can see it more clearly—like a swirling mass, almost as if it's alive, pulsing and shifting in the air. It's moving quickly, and there's no mistaking its intent. I feel a cold wave of panic roll through me, but I force myself to stay calm for Olivia's sake.

Winston growls, his body tense, but he doesn't move.

The red energy halts just before the edge of the clearing, hovering there like a predator waiting to strike. It seems to pulse as if it's breathing then starts to expand, stretching outward in all directions, its form twisting unnaturally. It's almost like it's testing the air around us, searching for some weakness, some opening.

"Dad..." Olivia starts, her voice barely a whisper.

"Stay quiet," I whisper, keeping my eyes fixed on the glowing mass.

Time feels stretched and distorted as we wait for something to happen. My mind is racing, trying to figure out what to do, how to fight it or escape, but it all feels hopeless. The red energy seems unstoppable, and I have no idea how to defend us.

Then, as if responding to our presence, the swirling red mass suddenly lurches forward. My heart skips a beat, and I pull Olivia closer to me, wrapping my arms around her protectively.

This is it.

But just as quickly as it lunges toward us, a bright flash of blue light bursts from the ground beneath us, cutting off the red energy's path. I stagger back, shielding Olivia with my body as the ground trembles. The light grows in intensity, pushing against the red energy, forcing it back into the trees.

The red mass sways, like a creature recoiling from a blow. Then, with an angry hiss, it begins to shrink, pulling back into the forest, leaving only a faint, lingering glow in the distance.

For a moment, the clearing is silent, except for Winston's low growl, I take a deep breath, trying to steady my racing heart. The sense of danger fades, but the unease lingers.

"Is he gone, Dad?"

"I'm not sure. I think so."

"Mary saved us. Did you see the blue light? Did you?"

I nod then ease my grasp on her while still clutching her hand. "Let's get out of here."

Just as we're turning toward the narrow path, Olivia stops and points at a tree where the red eerie light last was, "Look. There's something on the bottom of that tree," she says, shining her flashlight on the trunk.

"I don't think now is the time to look at things. We should get out of here before anything else happens."

"No! I've got to see. Please, Dad. Just a quick look and we'll leave, I promise."

Olivia pulls me about ten feet from where we're standing to a tall Douglas Fir. "Look, she points to the bottom of the trunk. Look what it says."

Shine my flashlight at the bottom of the tree and take a step closer. I strain to make out the words, Thomas Cotton carved deeply in the bark.

"We found it! We found it! We found his grave!"

I sigh, "Olivia, maybe we should come back in the daytime and..."

"That's a terrible idea. You said it yourself, if we wander around in the daytime with shovels and start digging, someone might see us and call the authorities. Besides, Mary chased Thomas Cotton's spirit away, at least for now. I think we owe it to her to do what you agreed to and find his bones. She needs them to cast him away. If we go back to the cabin, he'll just show up again and when he does, he may do something horrible to me, something that you won't be able to stop." She bends down and grabs my shovel and then passes it to me, "Here. Let's just dig for a few minutes and if we don't find anything, we can go home."

I shake my head. This has bad idea written all over it.

Winston surveys the area around us as I kick down on the shovel and break into the hard earth. Olivia follows suit and grunts as she steps down on her shovel, doing her best to make a dent in the soil.

"I can't believe we actually found the grave!" Olivia says with a level of excitement.

"We don't know if someone just carved Thomas Cotton's name on the tree or if he was buried here." I look around after every shovel of dirt I dig, keeping my eyes peeled for any signs of the red spirit.

Olivia looks around for Winston then says, "I think he's chasing a little animal or something, Silly dog. I'm going to go and find him."

I hear the shovel strike the ground, and as I turn to look in the direction she's running, something catches my eye—a soft glow in the trees at the edge of the clearing, just above her. "Olivia. Stop!" I yell as I throw my shovel and sprint after her.

A powerful gust of air swirls around me as I try as hard as I can to run toward my daughter. "Olivia! Look up!" I holler, hoping that she'll look up at the red light approaching.

But she doesn't. Her eyes are fixated on Winston who is sniffing in the grass. "Olivia!" I scream; my voice instantly swallowed by the wind.

The only sounds I can hear is the whooshing of air around me and my heart beating rapidly in my ears. I'm only halfway across the grassy span, pushing against what feels like an invisible brick wall. Then, I see Winston lift his head and notice the red spirit, although I can no longer hear him, I see his mouth opening and closing and his body become rigid. Olivia finally looks up and sees the blood red ghost pulsating above her. She whirls around and looks at me, her eyes full of terror.

My heart sinks as I use every bit of strength I have to reach her. Olivia starts to run to me but the powerful wind is between us and is causing us both to move in slow motion. I watch in horror as the spirit closes in on my child, my every instinct screaming to reach her, but I am powerless, helpless in my struggle to get to her. Then, the evil red ghost crashes into Olivia, knocking her forward. She lifts her head and locks eyes with me as the demon drags her backward toward the dark woods. "No! Let go of her, you son of a bitch! Let go of my child!"

But my efforts are for naught as Olivia stares at me in horror as she is pulled further and further away.

Finally, my body gives out, and in sheer exhaustion, I collapse to the ground, sobbing. When I look up, Olivia is gone. All that remains is Winston, silently barking and jumping at the edge of the dark forest. "Please, God. Please bring her back to me."

Lacking the strength to stand, I crawl, clutching handfuls of earth and grass, desperately pulling myself toward where I last saw my daughter. Then, as suddenly as it came, the powerful wind fades, and the first sound I hear is Winston's frantic yelping and barking at the dark trees. I struggle to my feet, barely managing to stand when something speeds overhead. I look up just in time to see a dark blue orb with a white, pulsating center, zooming across the grass before disappearing into the trees. "Olivia was right, it's Mary. It has to be. For a brief moment I feel a slight pang of hope as I gather my footing and move in the same direction. It's only when I reach the distressed dog at the edge of the woods that all hope fades. I stare between the dark trees, searching for any sign of the spirits. But all I see is blackness—emptiness, a void staring back at me. I reach down and touch Winston, who has been barking so aggressively that he didn't hear me approach.

Winston momentarily stops barking until I take my first step into the thicket and he looks up into the trees and lets out a yelp. I look up to see a mixture of red and blue, woven together, violently churning among the trees and branches. Maybe Mary reached Thomas Cotton before he hurt Olivia, are the only thoughts in my head. I sprint into the darkness of the woods when I hear a faint sound behind me, as does Winston. We turn around to see Olivia standing on the opposite side of the clearing, her arms raised toward me. I blink a few times to make sure I'm not imagining her but when Winston takes off running toward her, I know she must be real. Rushing towards her through the thick brush, I run as fast as my body will let me toward my daughter. By the time I reach her, Winston is moving in circles around her.

"Olivia!" I say, grabbing her in my arms.

"Mary told me that we have to hurry. We have to keep digging."

I shake my head, tears rolling down my cheeks, "No! We're getting out of here now."

"We can't! Look!" Olivia points to where the spirits are fighting in the night sky. "She's trying to distract him but he's very powerful. If Mary fails, we fail and he will take me. I'm sure of it. We have to find his bones quickly!"

Olivia runs over and retrieves our shovels then hands me mine. "Hurry, Dad. Please!"

Switching into auto pilot, I follow Olivia back to where we had started to dig and with more force than before, both of us chop and dig at the earth.

After every few shovels, Olivia looks back across the field at the spirits then urges me to dig faster.

When I finally look down at the depth of the hole we've created, I would guess we've dug a pit about two feet deep. "I'm not sure if this is the right spot. Nothing seems to be, and then I hear the shovel scrape as it hits something hard in the bottom of the hole.

"Did you hear that, Dad?" Olivia throws down her shovel and kneels on the edge of the pit. "You've hit something." She gasps.

"It could just be a rock or a piece of root," I say, putting my shovel down and kneeling beside Olivia.

"I'll use my hands to dig just in case," she says.

"No. Move back a bit. I'll do it."

I reach down deep into the hole but all I feel is cold earth.

"Dig, Dad. Hurry."

I lay down on my stomach and with both hands paw rigorously at the dirt. It isn't long before I feel something. I can't see what I'm touching but the texture feels like stiff woven fabric and it's covering something. Something hard and unforgiving.

I tell Olivia to hand me a flashlight as I clear more soil.

"What's in there?"

"I'm not sure. I think it's a cloth bag or something." I say, reefing on the fabric.

"Hmm. I doubt it will be a body. I mean, it would have to be a pretty big..."

Without warning, the soil loosens and the fabric gives way. I pull out a filthy woven sack and it's not light, I'd estimate the bag or the contents to be upward of twenty pounds.

I tell Olivia to shine her light on the sack as I quickly open it, the fabric almost coming apart in my hands.

Tied with a thin leather strap, I slowly manipulate the knot and then toss the strap aside. As soon as the light shines through the top, I clearly make out what looks like a human skull.

"What is it, Dad?"

I reach over and grab the strap then re-tie the bag, grateful that Olivia didn't see what I did.

"Why did you do it up? What is in there?"

"It's what we came for." I say, standing up and brushing myself off."

I look up to the trees but can't spot the spirits anywhere. "Did you see them while I was pulling the bag out?"

Olivia shakes her head, "No. But I was too busy watching what you were doing.

Winston turns to look across the small field and starts to growl. Both Olivia and I look at each other, "It's time to go," we say, in unison.

As we make our way onto the narrow path carrying our supplies and the sack of human remains, Olivia asks again about seeing what's inside the bag.

"I told you already and you don't need to see an old skeleton just to appease your morbid curiosity."

"Fine!" Olivia snaps. "But I'm not trying to be morbid, it's just that I've never seen a real skeleton before."

"And you're not going to see one tonight."

Olivia huffs a few times then focuses her attention on Winston who is walking in front of us on the trail.

He's turned out to be a very useful addition to our family, especially through the encounters with the evil spirit. Though he may not be able to catch the ghost or even deter it, at least he lets us know when it's near.

Finally, we make it out of the woods and step onto the beach, heading toward home.

Suddenly, Olivia stops walking and stares out toward the water.

"Keep moving. I'm carrying a lot of stuff." I say.

"No. Dad. Look." She says, pointing straight ahead. "Is that Mary?"

I look around her to see a figure sitting on the beach looking out over the sea.

"We should bring her the bones now, dontcha think?"

I nod. Yes. But let me go. You and Winston stay here."

"But I've got to pee really bad." She protests.

"Then pee behind a log or in the bushes. I don't want you out of my site after what happened tonight."

I put down the shovel and cradle the bag of bones under one arm and tell Olivia that I'll be right back.

As I walk across to the beach toward Mary, I briefly glance back at Olivia to make sure she's in view. Once I get close enough, I notice that Mary is wrapped in something, an old woven blanket that is draped around her shoulders. Once I am beside her, I drop the bag to the ground. "Mary. I brought you what you asked for."

She doesn't look at me, instead, she keeps focused on the water.

"You were there in the woods tonight, weren't you?"

Mary nods.

"And it was you who caused the feathers to spin over to the tree. Am I right?"

Again, she nods.

"But I don't understand why if you knew where Thomas Cotton was buried, you didn't get the bones yourself."

"Because if I had unearthed him, without the protection of my family, he would have overpowered me."

"But you fought him away. I don't understand."

"I could protect you from him while you were gathering his bones, but If I had found his remains, his spirit would've connected with his bones and he would become more powerful, enough to take me with him to the dark side and once that happened, I would never be able to find my way home."

"Home? Where is your home?" I say, glancing back at Olivia who is drawing in the sand.

"Mary? Where is your home?"

She remains silent for a few moments before finally speaking. "Keep Olivia close tonight and pray that I am successful. Only then will you be safe."

I try to piece everything together. Why did she need the bones? What is she going to do with them?

"Will I see you again?" I ask, my voice uncertain, unsure of what else to say.

She nods but still won't meet my gaze. "Go now, Oliver," she says, her hand resting on the bag. "Take Olivia and don't leave the cabin until daybreak."

A cold shiver runs down my spine as her words sink in. Whatever she plans to do with the bones, it's clear it's something dangerous

— something that has her genuinely worried for our safety.

Knowing that Mary isn't about to answer any of my questions, I walk toward Olivia and Winston then wave at them and point to the cabin.

* * *

"Dad, I'm nowhere near tired, can we go to 7-11 and get some snacks?"

I shake my head, remembering how Mary told me to keep Olivia indoors until the sun comes up.

"I'm tired and I think we've both had a bizarre and exhausting night." Then, I suggest she rummage through the cupboard and find a snack.

She sighs as she ambles into the kitchen and opens the cupboard doors. As she searches, she says, "So, what did Mary say to you when you spoke with her on the beach?

Did she tell you what she was going to do with Thomas Cotton's bones?"

"No. I just handed her the sack. We said very few words to each other."

Olivia sighs with disappointment, "Do you think that she may need our help? We owe her a lot. After all, she did save me tonight." Olivia grabs a bag of chips then closes the cupboard doors with a bang before walking over to the couch and sitting beside me.

I shake my head, "No. Whatever she's planning on doing, I think that you and I would only be in the way. I think it's best that we stay inside and get ready for bed."

"What do you mean by stay inside? Did Mary tell you that? What about Winston? I'm still going to have to take him out for a pee."

"I'll take him out, not you."

"Why? I always take him out. You're not making any sense at all."

"Olivia," I say making eye contact. "Just this once don't argue with me, okay?"

"Fine!" she says, getting up and walking to her room.

"And don't forget, you and Winston are sleeping in my room tonight."

She answers with a mumble but I can't make out what she's saying. Taking her age into consideration, she's probably quietly protesting.

Getting up from the couch, I call the dog to go out for his last pee break of the night. Once he's next to me, I exercise caution, open the door and shine the flashlight around the dark yard, keeping Winston at bay until I know it's safe. With no visible sign of Thomas Cotton's evil spirit, I walk out on to the top step and motion for Winston to go pee and he dives off the stairs in a mad rush to find a bush and relieve himself. He quickly sniffs the foliage on either side of the driveway and then rushes around the house where I can't see him.

Shining the flashlight, I step down two stairs and wait for a long few moments then yell for him to come. I wait for another couple of minutes and there's still no sign of him. "Damn dog." I say under my breath before cautiously stepping onto flat ground in front of the car. "Winston," I yell even louder.

I'm just about to take another step toward the corner of the house when a giant gust of wind swoops up and pushes into me, almost knocking me off my feet. Instantly, I recall the power of the gust I felt in the woods earlier when the evil red spirit was dragging Olivia across the grass. He's here. My first instinct is to turn and make my way back into the house but I know I can't leave Winston out here alone. Mustering all of my strength, I push against the wind, using the house to brace myself and walk to the side of the house. There on the path is Winston, his fur blown flat from the intense wind as he manipulates his way toward me. Just as he approaches, I see a huge fiery flash zoom across the sky and shoot toward the beach.

Using all of my strength I get myself and the dog through the pushing wind and up the stairs. When I open the front door, the pressure from the gale slams it against the inside wall creating a hole from the doorknob.

After I manage to get the door closed, Olivia runs out of her room and down the hall, "What's wrong? What happened?"

I lock the front door and tell her to go to the front room and get on the couch. Once she and the dog are seated, I walk over to the window overlooking the inlet and see the fiery red light swirling over what looks to be a small fire on the shore.

"Shut the lights off, quickly." I say to Olivia.

Once the lights are off, I see a figure in front of the flames. It's Mary, it has to be. She is walking around the fire and tossing something into the flames. When whatever she's throwing hits the flames, sparks fly into the air.

"Is that Mary?" Olivia walks up beside me at the window.

"Yes. I'm sure it is."

We stand motionless, watching as Mary continues to walk around the fire with the glowing red energy twisting above the flames.

"Look, Dad. It's the evil spirit of Thomas Cotton! Mary is trying to banish him back to the spirit world."

I glance at her briefly.

"How do I know that?" Olivia says, crossing her arms. "I told you. I've read a lot about ceremonies involving evil spirits and stuff."

We turn back to the beach, watching as the flames rise higher, the red spirit hovering above, drawing closer. It feels like time slows as the spirit and the flames twist together in the air. We keep watching as Mary raises something larger, holding it toward the swirling fire before tossing it into the center of the blaze.

"That was the bag that Thomas Cotton bones were in. It was the same size and everything," Olivia says.

Suddenly, powerful white sparks appear at the center of the flames and shoot up into the night sky.

"Wow! Did you see that?" Olivia exclaims. "It looked like there were fireworks coming out of the fire."

I turn to her and nod just as a mighty thud hits the window. Olivia screams as I look through the glass at the beach. The fire is now out, there's not even the sign of an ember or a trail of smoke.

"That's so weird." Olivia says staring at the beach. "How could the tall flames burn out so quickly and where's Mary gone?"

"I don't know." I'm concerned for Mary, maybe something happened to her while she was throwing Thomas Cotton's bones into the flames, maybe he took hold of her and dragged her with him into the fire. I want to go and investigate but I can't. Mary told me to stay in the cabin until daybreak. If my daughter wasn't with me, things would be different. I would go to the beach and look for Mary but with Olivia's safety in mind, I can't risk it.

"It's bedtime," I say, motioning to the hallway.

Chapter Seventeen

It's noon when Olivia and I are woken by Winston whining to go outside. I sit up and look out the window, the sky is grey but the trees aren't moving which means the wind has died down. Olivia gets out of bed to let the dog out and I head to the bathroom to have a shower and get dressed.

Once I'm finished, I go to the kitchen and begin to make coffee just as Olivia is coming in the front door.

"Dad, we went to the beach where we saw Mary from the window last night and guess what?" she says.

I raise my shoulders. "What now?"

"Not only was Mary not there but any sign on the fire was gone too. There wasn't even a scrap of wood or ashes or anything on the sand."

"You're right, that is weird."

Perplexed, I finish making my coffee and think about what she just told me. I wonder if the tide came in and swept any evidence of the fire out to sea. That's the only reason why there would be no sign of the fire.

I take my cup and place it on the end table while Olivia and Winston trail off to her bedroom. They're not gone five minutes when Olivia returns, "Guess what? Grandma has a box of pictures of mom's and she's packed them up for me, isn't that great?"

I nod. "It's about time she let you have your mother's things. Is she dropping the box off?"

She nods.

When Olivia steps closer, I notice her face is ashen and her eyes have dark circles around them.

"How are you feeling?"

She shrugs, "Okay, I guess. My tummy was turning earlier but I think I'm feeling a bit better now."

I point down the hall, "Go jump into bed. You need more sleep. You look like you've caught a bug or something."

She sighs, "I must've caught something from the cousins at grandma's. The kids that were there said they were off of school because they were ill."

"Go and lay down. Sleep is what will make you feel better."

"But what about grandma? She's going to drop off the box soon and I want to thank her when she gets here."

I tell her that I will meet Greta and take care of Winston, too."

* * *

Seven hours pass, and Olivia is still sleeping. Greta dropped off the box about an hour ago, and when I went outside to meet her, I could tell she was in one of her typical moods. She just handed me the box, turned around, and got back in her car without saying a word or even asking to see Olivia. Classic cold Greta.

Winston whines at the door and I put my book down and quickly check on Olivia before taking him for a walk on the beach.

Once we've reached the sand, I unhook the dog's leash and let him loose. He sniffs at the ground then takes off running. While I follow him on the beach, I stop at the same spot the fire was blazing last night. Olivia was right, there's no remnants of a fire being lit at all.

I watch as Winston darts into the shallows of the water, only to back up when a wave rolls in. He repeats this over and over, charging forward and then retreating as the waves come toward him. Once I'm sure he's had enough exercise, I call for him to come to me. He starts to, but then something catches his eye on the shoreline, and he stops. I watch as he paws at the sand before sticking his muzzle into the water. When his mouth reappears, water draining from his chin, I notice something hanging from his mouth. I call him again, and this time, he responds, running toward me with his newfound treasure swinging from his muzzle.

Once he's within arms distance, he bends his head down in front of me and drops the item on the sand. I bend over to pick it up and see that it looks like some sort of jewelry, a necklace with a leather strap and a shiny colored pendant. Once I have it in my grasp, I take a closer look, it's an abalone shell that's shaped like a teardrop. Examining the cracked and weathered looking leather strap, I can tell it is very old. As I hold the necklace up, letting the abalone shine, something occurs to me, "Could this be the same necklace that Mary has been incessantly searching for?

I stuff the old jewelry into my pocket and Winston and I head back to the house.

As soon as we get inside, I see Olivia laying on the couch with a glass of water in her hand.

"Feeling any better?" I ask.

She nods, "Much. I'm glad that I listened to you and went back to bed, though I still feel like I could sleep some more."

"I'll make you a can of soup from the cupboard and maybe you should stay in bed, either out here on the couch or in bed."

Before I know it, it's ten o'clock and I'm starting to feel a little sleepy. Though, I will myself to stay alert. I'm eager to see Mary on the beach tonight, first, so I can make sure she's okay after that weird fire spectacle she put on last night, and second, so I can show her the necklace and see if it's the same one she lost.

* * *

Ominous dark clouds roll across the sky consuming the wind. As I walk the path around the house I struggle to breathe the still air, and by the time I reach the edge of the sand I'm straining to draw full breaths. Ahead of me, standing motionless on the shore, Mary stares down the long span of beach. I make my way towards her, and I notice a gull flapping its wings as it struggles to take flight.

My feet crunch on the sand as I get closer to where Mary is standing.

"Are you okay?" I ask when I reach her side, but she doesn't look at me.

I reach into my pocket and pull out the necklace, dangling it in front of her. "Is this yours? Is this what you've been searching for?"

Mary raises her hand, trembling as her fingers close around the jewelry. She looks up at me, tears welling in her eyes. "I've searched for so many years to find this. Now, my family can find me. Thank you, Oliver. Thank you.”

She turns, her gaze fixed in the distance, unblinking.

“Mary,” I call softly, “What are you looking at?”

She raises a hand and points into the distance.

I scan the beach, trying to follow her gaze, but all I see are the white-capped waves crashing onto the shore.

“They’ve come to take me home,” she whispers.

“Who? Who is ‘they’?”

Her face grows ashen, her strength fading. She turns her eyes to mine.

“Without you, I would’ve been trapped here forever. Thank you, Oliver, for everything.”

Her words barely leave her lips before she collapses into my arms.

“What’s happening to you?”

"It's okay," she murmurs, her voice barely audible.

I hold her tightly, scanning the beach trying to see what she was watching. At first, all I see is the dark night sky and the waves rolling onto the shore. But then, slowly, a wave of color begins to form in the distance.

"What is that?" I whisper, transfixed by the strange lights.

"It won't be long now," she whispers, letting go of me and straightening herself.

Though she is clearly weak, she pulls her shoulders back and resumes watching the shifting colors down the beach. As she watches, she reaches out and touches my arm.

"Listen to my words, for they may be the last you'll hear me say."

I stare at her curiously as she gazes deeply into my eyes.

"I have a message from your wife, Laura."

A sudden breath escapes me, and my chest tightens. "You saw my wife?" A tear rolls down my cheek.

"She told me her death wasn't your fault. She wants you to know that she's at peace now, and that you should let go of the past and move forward with your life. She also asked me to tell you that Olivia is strong, and that you needn't worry. Give her the freedom to find her own way."

Tears now flow freely down my face. "Did she say anything else?"

Mary nods. "She wants you to know that you were her one true love, and that she will always be with you."

"Thank you," I say, overwhelmed by a wave of gratitude.

"Look," Mary says, pointing down the beach.

The shapeless hues are now taking form, and I can clearly make out the shapes of women, wearing straw hats and colorful shawls over their shoulders.

"Mary. Is that your family?"

She nods.

"Should I take you to them?"

"No. It's not time yet."

We watch as the group of women turn in unison, raising their hands high and facing the sea.

Then, the waters before them begin to recede, leaving a stretch of wet sand in their wake. I stare, astonished.

"It's happening," Mary says, causing me to look back at her. I notice a soft glow beginning to appear under her skin, her face is shining with a luminescent blue light.

"Mary! What is this? What's happening to you?"

"It's okay, Oliver," she smiles reassuringly.

We turn our attention back to the women. Now, I see a massive peak of water rising before them. I blink to make sure what I'm seeing is real—and it is.

Glancing back at Mary, I notice her hands are beginning to glow. Within moments, the light takes over her skin. She transforms from flesh and bone into a brilliant blue light, every detail of her still visible, as if she hasn't changed at all—except now, she's radiant.

"You're beautiful," I say, smiling at her.

She reaches out to touch me, and when her fingers graze my arm, I don't feel pressure—but a euphoric energy washing over me. We're locked in the moment, when suddenly, her head turns sharply down the beach.

"Oh no!" she cries.

I look to see a fiery red blaze forming in the sand between us and the women by the shoreline.

"It's him. It's Thomas Cotton."

The red spirit races toward us, and I stare at it as it takes shape. Soon, I see the form of a man—dressed in old-fashioned clothes: britches, suspenders, a tattered woven shirt, and a worn hat.

"He must not reach me," Mary cries.

Then, something catches my eye—a massive wall of water rising beside us. As the spirit draws closer, I stand protectively in front of Mary, the sound of soft chanting floating through the air.

Just as Thomas Cotton approaches, I hold my breath, terrified. Then, without warning, he stops, his gaze drawn to the giant wave. The chanting grows louder, almost overwhelming.

"Stay where you are, Mary," I whisper.

A shape forms within the massive wave. At first, I can't make it out, but then I see the large, white teeth.

Thomas Cotton lets out a grisly moan. "Noooo."

A mystical form begins to materialize—a massive killer whale, rising from the water. I can hardly believe my eyes as it grows at an incredible speed, towering over us.

"Noooo!" Thomas growls again, stepping backward from the water.

In a mighty roar of wind and sea, the creature opens its mouth and crashes down, the sound like thunder, swallowing Thomas Cotton's spirit whole.

I shake my head in awe as the massive wave of the whale sinks back into the sea, the air around us falling still. The women down the beach are now walking toward us, their singing growing louder as they approach.

Mary steps in front of me, then momentarily turns back. "Live your life well, Oliver. Find your peace."

I watch, tears filling my eyes, as Mary's radiant spirit walks weightlessly toward the clan. They merge into a breathtaking display of light. Together, they walk along the shoreline until they fade into a soft mist, and with a final sigh, they disappear completely.

Chapter Eighteen

The morning sun pours over Kitsilano, casting a golden glow on the beach as Olivia and Winston race ahead on the sand. I sip my coffee and stroll along behind them, glancing up at the balcony of our new home overlooking the water. It wasn't cheap, that's for sure, but with a dog now in the picture, the downtown penthouse just wasn't practical anymore.

The briny sea air fills my lungs, and for a moment, I let my mind wander to Laura—how she would've loved to see our life now. Olivia is thriving in a great school, making huge strides with her therapist, opening up about her feelings, and engaging in group conversations. She's excelling in her studies and seems well on her way to becoming a well-adjusted young woman.

I smile as Winston suddenly pauses to grab a mouthful of wet kelp, shaking it with vigor, splashing water and debris all over Olivia. "Yuck! Stop that!" she yells, laughing.

Some days, it's hard to believe we've come so far since our time in Comox. There are nights, though, when the house creaks or the dog barks unexpectedly during a storm, and I'll wake up to find Olivia curled up in her blanket beside me. I wish she could talk to her therapist about Mary and the evil spirit of Thomas Cotton, but I know she can't. A therapist wouldn't understand—they'd likely diagnose her with something that would stay on her medical record forever. So, we've learned that when those memories resurface, the only ones we can talk to about it are each other.

About a week ago, while we sat at the kitchen table having a late dinner, Olivia looked up at me with tears in her eyes and said, "I hope Mary is happy in the spirit world with her family." Then, she added, "If Mary hadn't been there when Thomas Cotton tried to take me, you might be sitting at the table alone."

The thought of losing Olivia hit me hard, and I felt tears welling up in my own eyes. I can't imagine life without her, especially after losing Laura. I reached out to hold her hand, reminding her, "No matter what life brings, good or bad, we'll always be stronger together than apart."

She smiled, wiped her eyes, and nodded, "Yeah, that's true, Dad. But we might not always be together."

I tilted my head, confused. "What could ever come between us?"

She hesitated, then looked down at the table. "Maybe one day, a boyfriend."

And just like that, reality set in. No matter what we've been through, no matter how close we are, I'm facing the inevitable— one day, my little girl will choose someone else over me. Probably some boy who is full of opinions and doesn't have a dime to his name. Then, there's that unimaginable day not far off, when Olivia will tell me she wants to spread her wings and move out of the house. The empty nesters club, a grim thought. Though, I admit, there's a part of me that could probably adjust to it—a life where I no longer have to clean toothpaste globs from the bathroom sink or deal with the stale food smell from dishes left in the living room overnight.

As for my future, I've been doing a lot of thinking. I never imagined a life without Laura in it, but now that she's gone, I'm forced to realign with who I was before I met her—the things I wanted to do. Traveling through Europe, maybe climbing the Great Wall of China, trips I dreamed about as a freshman in law school.

"Dad! Look, it's a seal!" Olivia exclaims; her voice full of excitement as she points to the inlet.

For now, though, I'll live in the moment and savor every minute of our unchanged life. I smile, take another long sip of my coffee, and walk toward my daughter.

The end

Jay Lang grew up on the ocean, splitting her time between Read Island and Vancouver Island before moving to Vancouver to work as a TV, film and commercial actress. Eventually she left the industry for a quieter life on a live-a-board boat, where she worked as a clothing designer for rock bands. Five years later, she moved to Abbotsford to attend university. There, she fell in love with creative writing and wrote five novel manuscripts in a year. She spends her days hiking and drawing inspiration for her writing from nature.

***Jay Lang books also published by
BWL Publishing***

Hush
Shatter
Shiver
Storm
The Cove
Impulse
The Immoral
Deadly Ties
Run Baby Run
Snake Oil
The Flying Dutchman
One Take Jake
One Take Jake: Last Call
Little Blue

www.ingramcontent.com/pod-product-compliance
Lightning Source LLC
Chambersburg PA
CBHW070057120726
47909CB00002B/419